NEXT LIFETIME

MONICA WALTERS

B. Love Publications

INTRODUCTION

Hello, Readers!

Thank you for purchasing and/or downloading this book. This is an EMOTIONALLY HEAVY read. It contains EXPLICIT LANGUAGE, LEWD SEX SCENES, and lots of MOMENTS OF DEPRESSION. It does not contain the typical HEA that you are used to from me, but there is a happy ending. If any of the previously mentioned offend you or serve as triggers for unpleasant times, please do not read.

Also, please remember that your reality isn't everyone's reality. What may seem unrealistic to you could be very real for someone else. But also keep in mind that, despite the previously mentioned, this is a fictional story.

If you are okay with the previously mentioned warnings, I hope that you enjoy the story of Nelsondra and Easton.

Monica

CHAPTER 1

elsondra

"You know, sometimes, I wish you would think before you speak. Some of the shit that falls out of your mouth can be offensive and hurtful."

"I was just joking, baby. I didn't mean anything by it."

"So, what exactly *did* you mean when you said, *And you expect ME to warm YOU up to sex wearing granny panties and warm-up pants.*"

"I didn't mean—"

"Naw! Don't tell me what you *didn't* mean. Tell me what you *did* mean and how I was supposed to take that!"

He stared at me with regret and sympathy in his eyes, but it was too late. I was crushed. My husband of fifteen years was, in so many words, saying that I didn't turn him on anymore. The tears left my eyes, despite my efforts to hold them in. Ever since I'd been diagnosed with neuropathy in my feet almost two years ago, things had been different. During sex, he had to do most of the work. I still gave him head, but lately, it seemed like we were even having disagreements about that. He felt like since I was practically *sexually disabled*, I should do what he wanted whenever he wanted me to.

Because I didn't want to give him head while I was on my period, I was wrong in his eyes. He didn't want to have sex while I was on my cycle. I didn't have extremely heavy periods, but he couldn't get with seeing blood or the different smell. That was fine with me. I didn't make a fuss about that even though I felt more sexual while I was on my period. But I didn't want to get all worked up sucking his dick, knowing I would get nothing in return.

We'd had a great day, shopping for paint. We had workers coming to our home in a couple of days to pressure wash the house and garage and replace some wood on our deck. All of that would need repainting once they were done. Things changed on the way back to my parents' house to pick up the kids. Somehow the conversation went left, and I didn't even remember how it got there... how we ended up on the conversation of sex.

Broderick was still standing there... not answering my question. "Baby, you know I would never intentionally hurt you. I was just joking."

"It doesn't matter what you meant. It hurt! And instead of you saying, *Baby, I'm sorry for making you feel like shit,* you're standing here trying to explain and make me feel like I'm overreacting. You know how I've been feeling lately. I'm not as confident as I used to be."

Truth was, I didn't feel beautiful or attractive anymore. I rarely ever wore real shoes. Most times, I wore house shoes because that was what was comfortable on my feet. The Lyrica only took the edge off the pain. Nerve pain had to be the worst. My feet literally hurt all the time. However, I was still able to function most days because I'd gotten used to it. I didn't work outside the home anymore, so I wore lounging clothes mostly. And because I couldn't really wear shoes without being in pain, I rarely dressed up.

We'd had this conversation a few times before. One time, he was complaining that I didn't seem into having sex and he would rather not have sex with me if I was gonna act like I didn't want to. So, I had to break it down for him. I really *didn't* want to, but I didn't want to turn him down. I thought we'd resolved our issues then. I'd told him that if I was hurting or didn't feel like it, then I would start turning him down. That was actually the second time we'd had that argument.

So, with him knowing my position... knowing how I felt about not being able to do the things I used to... him saying those words pierced my heart and I didn't know if I would be able to come back from them emotionally. "Nelly, you know I love you. You turn me on. My dick is always ready when we're about to have sex."

For all I knew, he could be thinking about someone else. Nothing was wrong with my pussy. She stayed wet as ever, even when I was in pain. She had her own mind and wanted it all the time. It was just that physically, I couldn't handle him even touching my legs or holding them up for an extended amount of time. The pain was getting worse and was traveling to my legs. At this point, I just wanted to be done with it all. "I don't wanna talk about it anymore."

"You wanna just forget about it? Like, go on like this didn't happen?"

"Yes."

It seemed that there was nothing I would be able to say to make him understand how I was feeling. How could he tell me how to feel about something he said? He wasn't me, but now he had me analyzing myself like something was wrong with me. Maybe there was. I felt like I was in despair and I didn't know how to pick myself up. I'd always been the strong one emotionally and mentally, but now I felt like my world was crumbling around me. My self-love seemed to be dwindling and I hated that feeling.

I began playing on my phone while he stared at me. "Nel, I'm sorry."

I waved him off. I was done talking about how I felt. It felt like I was talking to an invalid when I tried to explain myself. I was better off keeping my feelings to myself as I always did anyway. No one cared how I felt. I was the dumping site. They dumped all their problems and issues on me because I could handle the weight, but eventually, it got heavy. Where was I supposed to dump it? All their weight and weight of my own... it was just so heavy. It was no wonder I wasn't getting any better.

My diabetes was out of control and that was probably why my feet were hurting so badly. Stress was real and it was affecting my health in ways I couldn't explain. And now... my feet were killing me. I sat in my dad's recliner and put my feet up, exhaling loudly, glad that they hadn't made it back with the kids. "I'm gonna head home since you're dismissing me anyway."

He walked out, heading to his truck. I was already here when he'd gotten off work. So, we had two vehicles here. I let the tears fall from my eyes. I was feeling so broken, but I had to suck it up before the kids got back. They were extremely attentive to me and knew when something was wrong. Going to the bathroom, I wet and rung a towel and laid it on my face, then took deep breaths. My heart rate finally started to slow down, and before I could get back to my seat, I heard my parents and the kids come through the door. They had my nephews and niece with them, too. I didn't know how they managed with six kids at the park, three of them ages five, two almost three, and one. "Mommy, we had fun! But it's hot! I gotta sit in here to cool off for a minute."

That was my nine-year-old. Always the grown-up. My eight-year-old had gone the opposite direction. She was a typical kid. "So, did the little ones behave?"

"Yes, ma'am. They were good."

I nodded, then went back to my phone, still trying to get my thoughts subdued. "Nel, we have pizza if you want some."

"Maybe in a lil bit. Thanks."

My appetite was long gone. Broderick and I were supposed to get something to eat on our way back here, but after the conversation changed, so did our destination. I hadn't eaten all day and I felt a headache coming on. Continuing to play on my phone, I received a text message. *I'm sorry for hurting you. I love you. Hope you can forgive me.*

I quickly exited out of it. I didn't want to start crying again, so I ignored him. After the kids ate their food, they were ready to go play. My oldest daughter wanted to show my sister the routine she made up for Megan Thee Stallion's "Savage" remix with Beyoncé. As my phone played the song, we watched her tick-tock her hips. We laughed and rooted her on until my phone rang. It interrupted her routine and I didn't want to answer it. My daughter answered on speakerphone instead. "Hey, Daddy."

"Hey. Where yo' mama?"

"Right here."

Because I didn't want my kids, sister, and mama to know that something was wrong, I answered. "Yeah?"

"Should I throw these leftovers away in the fridge?"

I rolled my eyes. That was his way of initiating conversation with me. He knew I was pissed and hurt. When I was that way, I refused to talk to him. "Yeah."

"Huh?"

I suppose the background noise was too loud. "Yes! Throw them away."

"Okay."

I ended the call, and when the music resumed, my daughter went back to her routine. We applauded her when she was done, then they went back to playing. I sat quietly, watching them play a ball game, wishing I could enjoy playing with my kids. Because of the pain in my feet, I tried to do minimal physical activity when I wasn't at home. It was impossible to get totally comfortable when I was somewhere else. Plus, they were starting to swell at times. I hated taking medicine. I was already injecting myself five times a day with insulin and had been for almost twenty years, before I knew Broderick existed. But now I was taking Lyrica for the nerve pain three times a day, Metformin at night to assist the insulin, and a low dosage of something for my blood pressure at night.

It was a lot. My feet were developing discolorations on them that resembled "liver splashes" and no one could tell me what they were. I vaguely remembered seeing them on my grandmother when I was a kid. Thoughts of her made me nervous. Made me feel like my life was mimicking hers. She died at the age of sixty-six. The only difference was that my issues started a lot earlier than hers. Diabetes barged its way into my life when I was twenty-two or twenty-three. Living with it was challenging, especially with having children and a husband that never educated himself on the disease.

After watching the kids play outside for nearly two hours, I was ready to just go home and take a shower, then go to bed. Standing from my chair, I walked inside to tell my dad and brother-in-law goodbye, then ushered the kids to the car. "Mommy, can you watch a movie with us when we get home?"

"After we all shower, yes."

"Yay!" they both yelled in excitement.

There went going to bed, but it was the least I could do to spend quality time with them. Although my head was pounding, I'd take two Tylenol and deal with it... as I always did.

CHAPTER 2

E aston

THIS DAY COULDN'T DRAG ANY MORE THAN IT ALREADY WAS. I WAS scrolling through Facebook, waiting for the last thirty minutes to end. Sitting here waiting for someone to be brought to F&I was like waiting for my life to end. Things had been slow here at the dealership, but today was *extremely* slow. I'd caught up on all my work and made sure all my problem car deals had proper notes on them. There was nothing left to do. As I scrolled, I caught a glimpse of a familiar face. Backtracking, I noticed it was in the *people you may know* section.

When I saw Nelsondra Allison, I got excited. We were cool in high school and I always had a slight interest in her, but we'd both gone through school, entertaining other people. We were really good friends... close as hell. We would clown together in biology class and we sat next to each other in economics. Going to her profile, I saw that she was living here in Beaumont. I friend requested her, then scrolled her page. I knew she'd left town to go to school, but I didn't know that she'd come back. *She was married with two kids.*

Damn. While my interest was piqued, thinking I would have a shot, I accepted that, once again, I'd missed my opportunity. I'd never gotten married. After college, I'd gotten engaged, but ended up breaking it off. I was only engaged because everyone else thought Jana was right for me. After finally gathering the nerve, I ended our engagement. She wasn't the one. While I loved her, I felt no excitement... nothing. Just... the feeling wasn't there... the chemistry seemed forced. I'd been single ever since, occasionally dipping into something just to fulfill my sexual cravings.

Getting my lunch bag, I closed out Facebook and left my office, headed to my car. By the time I got there, my mama was calling, but I didn't even feel like entertaining her shenanigans at the moment. She was always trying to hook me up with somebody from church. She was the reason I joined a whole 'notha church. I'd been on several dates with women she set me up with that were a waste of time. Before I could take off, my phone chimed, alerting me of a message. It was Facebook messenger. When I saw Nelsondra's name, I got excited. Opening it, I read, *Eeeeeaaast! What's up, big headed nigga? LOL*

I couldn't help but laugh. She was still the same. I didn't know how we lost contact, but I was glad to be in touch again. I messaged back, *Nellyyyyy! How you doing, baby girl?*

Cranking my engine, I decided to head home for the evening. It was hot as hell, and if Nelly messaged back, I'd just respond when I stopped again. Seemed like when it was slow at work, I was even more tired than what I would have been had I had customers back to back. I only lived a good five minutes from the dealership. As I drove, my mama called again. Rolling my eyes, I answered, "Hey, Ma."

"Hey, baby. You had a good day?"

"It was okay. How you doing?"

"I'm good, but I would be even better if you came by."

"I'm exhausted, Ma. Can it wait until tomorrow?"

"I guess so. Guess who I'm friends with on Facebook?"

I rolled my eyes again. She was on Facebook just to see what she could see. She rarely made a post, but she was in everybody's statuses and profiles, updating me on the happenings from Port Arthur to Houston and everywhere in between. Shaking my head slowly, I asked, "Who?"

"Nelsondra."

That was probably why she showed up in the people I may know. We had a few friends in common, but when she friended my mother, their algorithm connected her to me. "Yeah, I friend requested her a few minutes ago. I hadn't seen her in years."

"Mmm-hmm. You know she's married."

"I know, Ma. Nelly and I have never been nothing more than friends."

"I know, but I'm yo' mama, boy. I know you had a thing for her. Lie if you want to."

As I turned into my driveway and pulled into my garage, I said, "I did. But that was then. I'm almost forty-one years old. That ship sailed a long time ago."

"Okay. If you say so. Make sure you come get your food tomorrow. I wanted to surprise you with dinner, so you didn't have to cook, but it will be leftovers now."

"What did you cook?"

"Baked chicken, mustard greens, rice, and baked beans."

"What made you cook all that?"

"Aww, that ain't nothing. Just come and get it tomorrow."

"A'ight, Ma. I appreciate it. I'm 'bout to head in the house. I'll talk to you tomorrow."

"Okay. Love you."

"Love you, too."

When I got out of the car, I headed inside and went straight to the fridge for a Cayman Jack, then flopped on the couch. I'd put a roast in the slow cooker before I left this morning. A brother had learned from the best... my mama. I knew how to throw down in the kitchen. Her reason for teaching me to cook was that she couldn't have me out there looking like a spoiled mama's boy. My dad was never in the picture. We knew one another, but we'd never really spent time together... that I could remember anyway. My mama claimed he was around until I was three or so.

Despite the fact that I was a boy who loved being outdoors and playing sports, she taught me how to wash my clothes, cook, and clean. She said it was important that I knew how to take care of myself. I was appreciative that she went the extra mile with me. She taught me how to clean well, too. Not that surface shit most men do. I mean, baseboards, the bottom sides of the toilet, the grout in the tile... all that shit. Finishing off my drink, I went to the kitchen to fix my food. As I did, my phone alerted me of a message. *Nelsondra.* I opened it to read, *Sorry for the delay. I'm doing okay. A few health issues, but nothing debilitating. How have you been?*

I wondered what type of health issues she was dealing with, but I wouldn't dare ask. If she felt comfortable enough, she would say. We hadn't talked to one another in like twenty years. *Damn.* That was a long-ass time. I responded, *I've been good, just living.* I wanted to say more, but I didn't want to push for conversation. She could have been busy. Nel had a whole family to take care of. I had all the time in the world.

After sitting at the table to eat, she sent another message. *Well, are you married? Any kids? What do you do? Are you in Beaumont? Give me the juice. You acting like we strangers.*

Smiling slightly, I responded, *I didn't want to take up your time. I saw that you have a family to tend to. I'm not married, and I don't have any kids. I'm still in Boremont, as we used to call it, and I work at Classic Chevrolet as a finance manager.*

Going back to my dinner, I set the phone down, wondering about her. She seemed like the same person from high school, but that wasn't possible. It had been twenty years. We had all matured... changed in some way. After savoring a couple of bites, I went back to my phone when it chimed. *That's great! Are you dating? Or are you just chilling? I friended your mom today. It's so good to see she's doing well. God, I didn't realize how much time had gone by since I talked to you. How did we stop talking? We used to talk every day.*

I was starting to get a little antsy. I wanted to ask her out to lunch so bad. *She's married.* Messaging was cool, but I'd much rather talk in person. *She's married.* Maybe if I gave her my phone number, she could call whenever she had time. *She's married, nigga.* My conscience was beating my ass up. Deciding to reply, I typed, *I'm not dating. My mama told me y'all were friends on Facebook a little while ago. I'm not sure exactly how we stopped talking. You prolly met somebody and said, fuck East, I got bigger fish to fry.*

She immediately sent the eyeroll emoji, then followed it with the side-eye emoji. I was almost sure that was what had happened. We were too close back then. It seemed like it might have been gradual, but we fell off big time. She'd met my mama and I'd met her family, including her siblings. She had two sisters and a brother. Her brother was only like four or five when we graduated. I glanced down at my phone to see the side-eye again, then a laughing emoji. That was exactly what happened.

Finishing off my food, she sent another message. Man, I'd talk to her all night, but I wasn't up for causing confusion. She'd sent, *Well, don't be a stranger. I work from home, so I'm more available than not.*

I was dissecting that last line in my mind. Maybe I was reading too much into it, but it seemed like she wanted me to initiate more conversation. I simply responded with, *Aight, baby girl.*

As I put my leftovers in containers, all I could think about was Nelly. So, I went to her profile on Facebook and scrolled her pictures. She was still beautiful, and through her conversation, she seemed like the same crazy but friendly person she'd always been. Her daughters were beautiful as well. When I came across a picture of her and her husband, I noticed her smile wasn't as bright as it was in the pictures with her children or the pictures with anyone else.

I went through every picture and never once did I see a huge smile on her face. She was unhappily married and searching for someone to bring what she needed to her life. *Easton, nigga quit dreaming.* Putting my phone down, I turned on the shower, getting ready to get in. While I didn't do shit, I still needed a shower. It felt like I had the dealership stench on me.

Hopefully, tomorrow would be a much busier day than today. It was draining to sit there most of the day like that. I'd only had two customers the entire ten hours I was there. On a good day, there would be customers waiting in the waiting area for the next free finance manager. Nowhere near the case today. We were starting a new promotion with one of the local credit unions, so that should bring people in. No notes, no interest for six months. They would jump all over that.

Once I got out of the shower, there was another message. It simply read, *Goodnight*.

I chose not to respond because I didn't know if it was cool to do so. She'd sent the message almost fifteen minutes ago. Swallowing hard, I changed my mind and responded anyway. *Goodnight, beautiful.*

The pet names were something we always did. So, it wouldn't be unusual for her to read that. Although we clowned around a lot, we were good friends. When she experienced her first heartbreak, I was there consoling her, even though I had a girlfriend at the time. It was no secret that Nelly and I were close, and everyone respected that, even whoever my girlfriend was at the time. *Why didn't you go for it back then?* I was stupid and superficial. Nelly was always on the thick side and back in my teenage years, I went for the small waist and fat ass... the shit that was glorified on TV.

Now that I'd grown the fuck up, I knew how to appreciate women of all sizes, complexions, and shapes. Now, I mean, I still liked what I liked, though. Her looks had to attract me, of course. Nelly had always been beautiful. I was just with the shits back then. Once I got in bed, my phone chimed. I knew it was from her. Confirming my suspicions, I opened the app to read, *I'm not that beautiful anymore, East. Diabetes is tearing my body down.*

At that moment, I wanted to pull her in my arms, just like I used to do, and kiss her head, letting her know that everything was gonna be okay. I knew nothing about diabetes, other than most people who had it, had to change their lifestyle... everything about it, but especially their eating habits. I really didn't know what to say, but I said the first thing that came to mind. *You are extremely beautiful, Nelly. I'm sure your husband thinks so as well.*

She immediately sent the eyeroll emoji. Just as I thought. He wasn't being what she needed. She hadn't responded other than the eyeroll. *Nelly, what's going on? Just because we haven't talked in a long time doesn't mean that anything has changed.*

As I laid in the bed, waiting for her response, I started thinking of all the ways I could make her feel like she was the most gorgeous woman in the world. But I also hated that she even felt that way. Why wasn't her husband helping her through this? And why was she even with him if he wasn't? She responded saying, *I have nerve damage in my feet and it's spreading to my legs. I'm in pain most times. It's taking a toll on my marriage. I can't do all the things I used to do and I'm so stressed, it's only making the pain worse. I didn't want to lay all that on you, East. That's all my issues and I'm dealing with them the best way I know how.*

And what way is that?

I really felt for her now. Not only was she in physical pain, but she was in pain emotionally and mentally, too. She responded, *Right now, by talking to you.*

She had my heart tripping. *But why, though?* She was using me to make herself feel better. I was someone that she was used to that used to be her sounding board. Responding to her, I typed, *What were you doing before now? Can you call me?*

I was tired of texting or messaging on this shit. I would much rather talk than type all this shit out. *I spend time with my daughters. And yes. What's your number?*

After sending my phone number, I laid in the bed, waiting for her call, knowing that she needed a friend. *But could I handle that?* Only being a friend to her once again might be too much for my mental. I was a grown-ass man that knew what he wanted. I wanted Nelly. *She's married.* She's unhappily married. Whether it was happily or unhappily, it didn't change the fact that she was married. Could I respect its sanctity? Only if she did.

CHAPTER 3

N elsondra

"I'M NOT HAVING SEX WITH YOU, BRODERICK. BESIDES, I'M wearing sweats and a t-shirt. I'm surprised you're even turned on."

He huffed loudly. "I thought we were done with that."

"Just because I don't wanna talk about it, doesn't mean I'm done with it internally. I don't think you realize just how much you tore me down. I'm not having sex with you until I'm good and ready."

"Are you serious?"

"Hell yes!"

He rubbed his hand down his face. "So, you think you don't turn me on."

"Isn't that what you said?"

"No! Why you... fuck it."

It had only been a couple of days since Broderick had said those hurtful words to me, but I was supposed to move on from them like nothing had ever happened. That was what I wanted to do, but my feelings wouldn't allow that. I was still angry... hurt. Needing someone to talk to was important and I didn't have that until my best friend from high school suddenly friend requested me. The problem with that was that this best friend was a man. Broderick was so damn jealous and insecure, he would automatically think I was fucking around on him.

After I'd messaged Easton Bridges, trying to catch up with him and letting him in on my pitiful life, he wanted me to call him. I said I would, but then I decided against it. He never messaged back to ask why I hadn't called. It had been a couple of nights since then. I rolled my eyes and sat on the bed, bringing my hands to my face for a minute. This was too much. I wished Broderick would just leave already. He had to work tonight and was busy trying to get a taste. He still had yet to understand how I was feeling, and I was done with trying to explain it.

Easton would understand every moment... every feeling... he always had. Those thoughts made me wonder why I never pursued anything with him. However, none of that mattered at this moment. Broderick was the man I loved, and besides his thoughtless blunderings, he was a good man. It was like he had brain farts where he didn't understand how hurtful the things he said could be. But those moments killed me emotionally, especially towards him. Sometimes, I wanted to think that he knew exactly what he was doing to me and that he was playing me for a fool.

Why was I still here? Even working from home, I earned enough to take care of my babies alone. The Hilton afforded me almost four thousand a month after taxes. That was enough to afford a two-bedroom apartment, my car note, and insurance. Plus, I would definitely file child support on his ass. That would take care of food and other things the kids needed. But... I still wasn't sure if I wanted to give in just yet. So, if I wasn't sure, I felt like I should stay until I *was* sure. The kids weren't suffering. He was a great dad. Most times, he was better to them and treated them with more respect than he did me... took their feelings into account before he did and said things. Why couldn't he do the same for me?

Broderick came back in the room, fully clothed, about to leave for work. "I'm sorry I walked out the way I did. I wanna work

through this, baby. I'm trying. But you have to give me something."
He grabbed my hand. "Please, Nelly?"

"I'm just hurt."

"But you have to feel that I love you, right?"

"What are you doing to make me feel it?"

"I..." He looked away and released my hand as he thought about it. Looking back at me, he said, "I'll do better. I love you and I want you to feel it, Nel."

I took a deep breath and nodded. After kissing my forehead, he walked out, heading to work. I could hear him telling the girls bye as he headed out, then I heard them giggling. It wasn't that I was jealous of the relationship he had with the girls, but I wanted to experience that side of him, too. The side of him that was sensitive and caring. I experienced his humor all the time and that was great, but I needed more. When I heard the backdoor close, I glanced at my phone.

As soon as his truck cranked up, I grabbed it and messaged Easton. *East.* I still didn't feel comfortable using his cell phone number, so I sent the message through messenger. *Hey East. I'm sorry I didn't call. Things got a little hectic around here. How are you?*

I fought the urge to send it for a moment, then I sent it anyway, hoping he responded to me. We were so close in high school. I remembered exactly when we stopped talking. I was at Spelman in Georgia and I'd met Broderick. We were only friends at first... just hanging out. When I found out he was from Houston, I gravitated towards him, forgetting all about my friend. We were only texting every other day, sometimes every two days at that point. I'd invested my all into Broderick and it paid off. We fell in love and once we graduated, we got married.

I was diabetic back then when I met him, but it was at the beginning of my diagnosis. I had only been diagnosed a year before I met him. So, on the outside, I looked to be in great health. But here I was, almost twenty years later at forty-one years old, looking like I was one foot in the grave. Lying back in the bed, I picked my feet up as my phone chimed. Looking at it, I saw it was a message from Messenger. *Hey. It's cool. I'm good. What about you?*

Taking a deep breath, I typed out, *I'm good, too.*

I rolled my eyes and shook my head as I sent it, knowing that I wasn't good. My feet were swollen again. The fluid pill I'd been prescribed wasn't working. I was going to the bathroom more, but it obviously wasn't getting all the fluid off me. I was scared. It made me wonder if my kidneys were starting to fail. Had they taken all they could take? Most people in my family didn't make it once they were on dialysis. My grandmother, a couple of cousins, and an uncle all died a couple of years after starting. My father-in-law was on dialysis and his blood pressure frequently dropped on him to the point of him blacking out. I couldn't leave my babies. They were only eight and nine. They needed me.

My phone chimed, getting my attention, taking me away from my pity party. *You're a liar. Just because a lot of time has passed doesn't mean I don't know you anymore, Nelly. Something's wrong. Call me.*

I didn't want to call him. *Yes, I did.* But I couldn't. *Why? It was innocent.* It didn't feel innocent. I felt like I was cheating. Although East was my friend long before I met Broderick, it felt like I was trying to establish something with him. *Girl, East don't want your broke down ass.* I closed my eyes, trying to rid myself of my thoughts as my phone chimed again. *You're obviously uncomfortable with calling me. Why? You will always be special to me, Nelly. So, don't trip on that. We can talk here. What's up?*

Suddenly, I didn't feel like talking about my issues. I didn't want to weigh him down with my troubles. Leaving Broderick would be harder than hard, and I had no intention of doing so anyway. So why weigh him down with my issues if I wasn't going to do anything about it to remedy myself of them? I messaged, *How has work been?*

I rolled my eyes. I shouldn't have responded at all, but something inside of me needed to just talk... have easy conversation to help me forget about my problems. But deep down inside, I needed his sensitivity and attention where it mattered most. *I get it, Nelly. Work is good. It's work. What do you do?*

I smiled. That was what I loved about him. He understood me. East was my best friend and this moment made me realized why. He was always thoughtful and accepting of my feelings. *To hell with it.* I scrolled up in our thread and clicked on his number, calling him. After a couple of rings, he answered, "Hello?"

"I work for Hilton from home, accepting reservations. Hey, East."

"Damn! Hey, Nelly! What made you call?"

"Because I realized that I was tripping."

"Hell yeah. But as always, you come to your senses eventually if I let you be."

I laughed and so did he. Once we stopped laughing, we remained quiet for a moment, listening to all the things the other one wasn't saying. We used to do that all the time, too. Finally, he broke the silence and said, "Why are you staying if you aren't happy, Nelly?"

"Because I love him. He's a good provider and father. We've only started having issues since I've been sick."

"What's wrong?"

"I'm diabetic. I've been diabetic for almost twenty years."

"Yeah. I remember when you were diagnosed."

I took a deep breath, then revealed, "I have neuropathy in my feet. They hurt all the time and my legs have begun to hurt as well. Most of our arguments have been about the things I can't do anymore."

"Things like what?" he asked softly.

"Just... things."

"Sex?"

I remained quiet and I heard him exhale. "You know I know about your sex game. Jeremy used to run his mouth and I had to pop him in it."

"Ugh! I forgot about that. I'm always turned on, it's just that at times when I'm hurting, I don't feel like it."

"What does he do to help soothe you? Does he rub your legs or your feet?"

"No," I said sadly. "He works a lot."

"If he has time for sex, he has time for that. But I don't wanna continue to down talk your man. I don't know him. You know you can always talk to me, Nelly. If you don't want me to say a word, I won't. I'm a good listener."

"I know, East. I missed you. For real."

"I missed you, too, baby girl. How's your family?"

"Everyone's good."

"Good. So, umm... where's your husband now? Would he be cool with you talking to me?"

"Not at all, but I know you know that. He's at work."

"So, I should always let you call me. Noted."

We were quiet once again. I knew it was my fault. I wasn't the comfortable, loud ass with him that I used to be. Things felt different between us. Maybe because we were much more mature now and had lived life. Whatever the case may have been, just as I was about to tell him goodnight, he asked, "Why are you so quiet? I know it's been a while, but I'm still the same ol' East."

"But I'm not the same ol' Nelly. I've been through some things and the latest has me so unsure of myself. I can't wear a shoe, East. You know how embarrassing that is? Then my husband told me in so many words that I didn't turn him on. That shit felt like somebody gut checked me. He swears that he didn't mean what he said that way, but I don't know how else I'm supposed to feel."

I was crying and had literally broken down on the phone. He was completely quiet while I talked, and I felt horrible for even letting that out. "I'm sorry. That wasn't supposed to come out. I have to go."

"Please, don't hang up, Nelly," he pleaded.

I held the phone, crying, not being able to silence the whimpers. "You probably don't need to hear this right now, but you've always been attractive to me. I wish I could hold you right now like I used to. I'm so sorry you feel that way. But even at what you feel is your very worst, you are beautiful to me. Remember that time we fell asleep on the floor watching a movie?"

I chuckled because I knew where he was going with this story. "Yeah. My hair was everywhere, and I had dried slobber on my face when I woke up."

"You were beautiful even then."

"Stop that damn lying! You clowned me for weeks about that!"

I laughed and he did, too. "I was supposed to clown you! But you were still beautiful, Nelly."

"If you were attracted to me, why didn't you ever ask me out?"

"Because we're friends. I didn't want to make you uncomfortable, plus I was too busy chasing hoes."

"Yeah, that last part was the real reason."

He laughed and said, "You prolly right. But if I could do it all over again, things would be different."

"No they wouldn't. You didn't like big girls. I'm even bigger now. But that's okay because I've started exercising a bit, trying to get slim like a bicycle rim."

He laughed loudly and I had to chuckle, too. "You crazy as hell. That's that superficial shit, though. I don't give a damn about your size. You're beautiful inside and out and please don't let anyone make you feel differently. I don't care who they are."

I closed my eyes for a moment, then said, "Thank you, East. For the record, I liked you back in high school, too, but I didn't think you had taken a second look at me."

"Damn. I really wish I could go back now."

I felt all warm inside. Easton was definitely flirting with me. I knew this had gone beyond him trying to make me feel better. "Easton..."

"Oh shit. You done called me Easton, so come with it."

I closed my eyes and slowly shook my head as I smiled. "I'm married and you're flirting with me."

"You right. I'm sorry, but I had to let you know how I felt about you."

I frowned slightly. "How do you feel about me now?"

"That you were made for me. That I missed out on something special."

"After twenty years?"

"I know. I sound stupid, like I'm playing on your emotions. I would never do that, Nelly. I apologize. But hearing you cry hurts my heart."

"I have to go, East. I'm too vulnerable right now. Hearing your voice makes me reminisce and think about things I shouldn't be thinking. I'll hit you up on messenger maybe tomorrow."

"I'm sorry. I really am. I wasn't trying to make things more difficult for you. Can I message you before you message me?"

"No. I'll reach out first."

"Okay. Have a good night."

"You too."

I ended the call and put my face to the pillow and screamed. I couldn't get caught up that way. Easton had never openly expressed an interest in me. I supposed time changed a lot of things, but I wasn't a cheater. Just talking to him made me feel guilty. Standing from the bed, I yelled to the girls that I was about to take a shower. After turning it on, I got undressed and looked down at my swollen feet. Dragging my hands down my face, I exhaled loudly, then got in and let the hot water wash my guilt away.

CHAPTER 4

E aston

I KNEW I SHOULDN'T HAVE EXPRESSED MY TRUE FEELINGS TO NEL, but when she started crying, I was hoping that it would make her feel better. That was so stupid of me. It had been an entire week and I hadn't heard a word from her. I wasn't the friend she needed. I was a lame-ass nigga that looked to be using her vulnerability to my benefit. That wasn't what I was doing. I was trying to let her know that her insensitive jackass that she called a husband wasn't the be-all end-all. I was sure he had fucking flaws that had nothing to do with his health.

They were the ones who belittled women like they were fucking perfect and had shit going on with them that their caring, compassionate partners didn't say a word about. I began scrolling Nel's Face-book page to see if I could get a glimpse of what he looked like. The last time I scrolled, I wasn't really paying attention to what he looked like. He was a big guy that was about her height, but other than that, I couldn't see any imperfections. I was pretty sure he had some, though. Everything in me wanted to reach out to her to make sure she was okay, but I didn't want to cause her any more trouble than I already had.

It was Friday, but since I had to work tomorrow, I decided to leave for lunch. Most times, I brought something from home and chilled out around the job. I needed a break away from this place today. It had been so busy I was late going to lunch. It was almost three and I was starving. As I headed out, I noticed a couple of ladies from the accounting office that I talked to at the coffee pot all the time. "Where y'all coming from?"

"We went to McAlister's."

"Was it packed?"

"Not at all."

"A'ight. Thanks."

I continued to my car and got in, heading five minutes away to McAlister's. I could go for a good sandwich. When I got there, I parked right at the door and quickly made my way inside out of the heat. I was thankful I worked in finance and not in sales because that heat wasn't playing. It felt like it was every bit of a hundred degrees in the shade. After getting inside, I ordered what I wanted, then took my iced tea to a corner table. When I sat, our eyes met. *Shit.* It was Nelly and she was with her husband and children.

I looked away, trying not to cause her to get caught looking at me, but I couldn't help but steal glances. She didn't look happy, but everyone at the table seemed to be oblivious to that fact. How couldn't her husband tell that something was clearly bothering her? Before I could look away, she waved. I smiled and waved back as her husband turned to see who she was waving at. He frowned slightly, so I stood from my seat and walked over to their table. What the hell, I felt invited.

When I got to them, I said, "Hey, Nelly! How you doing?"

"I'm good. East, this is my husband, Broderick, and my girls, Tiana and Zahria."

I shook her husband's hand, then waved at the girls as she

explained our connection. "East and I went to high school together and he gave me the blues all four years."

I twisted my lips to the side as her girls laughed. "We took at least one class together every year. And your mother tormented me."

Nelly laughed and her smile was just as beautiful as it was back in the day. The only thing I noticed that had changed was the weariness in her eyes. "No, seriously, he was my best friend. Granny and Grampy know him and so does your aunts and uncle."

"Why aren't y'all friends anymore, Mommy?" the daughter that she introduced as Zahria asked.

"Well, when we went off to college, we lost touch after I met your daddy."

So, she was admitting that he'd come between our friendship. I glanced back at him to watch him stare at Nelly, so I cleared my throat and said, "Well, it was good to see you, Nelly. Over twenty years is a long time. We gon' all have to hook up for lunch or something one day. Nice meeting you, girls, and nice meeting you as well, Broderick."

"Nice meeting you, too," he said unenthusiastically.

I smiled, then walked away as the waitress was sitting my sandwich down on the table. She looked around, then smiled at me. "If you need anything else, let me know."

"Thank you," I responded as I nodded.

When I sat, I caught Nelly's eyes once more. She was so damn beautiful, and I didn't understand what wasn't there to love about her. This woman had me smitten, and I couldn't stop glancing at her. When her husband stood from the table, the girls hopped up as well. Nelly grabbed her purse from the back of her chair as he walked away. One of her daughters waited for her and helped her from the chair. That alone pissed me off. When she stepped away from the table, I noticed the house shoes she wore. They were somewhat run-down, but he didn't seem to be lacking in his appearance, wearing a clean, fairly new-looking pair of cowboy boots.

Her daughter asked, "You okay, Mommy?"

That prompted me to look at Nelly's face, only to see her wincing as she tried to walk. She glanced at me and her face turned red as she said, "I'm okay, baby."

She continued to hold her hand and lead her away from the table. She smiled and waved at me and I waved back, feeling sorry for her. But because I knew Nelly like I did, I knew she wouldn't want me to feel sorry for her. But if he didn't even help her from her seat, he was a jackass. Where was the chivalry? Shit, where was the love he should have for his wife of over ten years? Man, how I would spoil her with attention and affection. He stood at the door, waiting for her, then opened the door for her and his daughters.

As I took a bite out of my sandwich, I shook my head. What he took for granted could be a blessing for someone else... someone else like me. But... I would back off. If she wanted to talk to me, she knew how to find me. I didn't care about all the physical ailments. I would take care of her like my life depended on it. Nelly's heart was gold and she was smart as hell. I knew that hadn't changed about her. I knew there would be no way her husband would take me up on my offer for us to do lunch, either. My eyes told everything, and I was almost sure my admiration for her had shown through them.

It took a strong person to deal with all that she was dealing with. Those physical ailments she had could take anybody down. I looked up neuropathy to find that nerve damage was constant pain. That was what neuropathy was. So her feet hurt all the time. I could imagine that some days were better than others, but today didn't seem to be a good day, just by the look on her face when she stood.

I finished eating, then headed back to work, hoping to get the day over quickly. My day was supposed to end at seven, but it could very well go longer. Trying to get some customers financed was tedious. If their credit score wasn't the best or they didn't have enough credit history, a lot of lenders refused to take a chance on them. If they did, the interest rate was out of this world. One time I'd ended up staying at work well after the closing time of eight. When I got home, it was nearly ten o'clock.

The five-minute drive back was consumed with thoughts of Nelsondra. I wanted to call her... message her... anything to talk to her. My heart was aching for her and I didn't know what to do about it. *She's married, East.* Regardless of how unhappy she may have been, she was still married, and I needed to pound that in my head. We would both only end up hurt, especially me.

When I got back to work, I parked in back and walked toward the building. However, my heart stopped when my phone chimed. I knew it was Nelly. I felt that in my spirit. Looking at my phone, I saw a message that read, *You look good, East. Time has been on your side.*

Taking a deep breath, I warred within myself about what I would say in return. I still had ten minutes left on my lunch break, so when I got to the shade of the building, I typed out, *These gray hairs in my beard say differently. You looked so beautiful, Nelly. Simply gorgeous. I wish I could have hugged you and pulled those braids.*

I knew she would know exactly what I meant by that last line. She'd gotten braids in her hair our junior year in school. Every time we would pass one another in the hallway, I would pull them, and she would curse me out. She didn't get braids again after that. My phone chimed and a smile played on my lips. *Thank you, jackass.*

I chuckled to myself, then headed inside the building to see several customers waiting to be seen by a finance manager. There went the rest of my day. At least I would be busy and not pining over Nel.

⚜

"Yo, what's up? You wanna go to Madison's for drinks?"

"Yeah. I'm just leaving work. I'll meet you there."

That was my boy Aaron from high school. We tried to hang out at least once a week. I needed to talk to him about Nelly. They used to argue nonstop in school, but they always had each other's back. I wondered if he'd talked to her since school. As I made my way to Madison's, I exhaled. I didn't know how to rid myself of thoughts of her other than at work. I was so busy, I didn't have time to think about her. It was after eight and I was just leaving. Tomorrow, I didn't have to come in until ten, so I was happy about that.

As I parked, I grabbed my phone. I pulled up my apps and saw the red number next to the messenger icon, letting me know I had new messages. Going into the app, I hoped there was a message from Nelly. She'd left the message an hour ago. It read, *I'm tired of this. What are you doing tonight? My mama is watching the girls.*

My heart rate sped up significantly as I typed out, *I just got off and I'm meeting Aaron at Madison's. You're welcome to join us.*

I could see the dots, indicating she was responding. *I'm on my way. See you in ten minutes.*

Shit, I didn't know if this was a good idea or not, but I was anxious to see her. I responded, *Okay beautiful.* Getting out of the car, I made my way inside to see if Aaron had arrived. As I looked around, he appeared behind me. "Looking for somebody?"

"Yeah. Let's get a table instead of sitting at the bar. Nelly is coming."

"Nelly? Nelsondra from high school?"

"Yeah."

"Damn! I ain't seen or talked to her ass in years. I can't wait to get cranked up tonight. I'm gon' be on her ass like white on rice."

I chuckled, then slid my hand down the front of my head, feeling the hairs tickle my palm. My sensitivity wanted me to tell him to be easy with her, but then I knew that Nel would know I told him to do so, so I decided against it. "She's married now."

"You sound like that bothers you. You still feeling her?"

"A lil bit."

"Naw, nigga! I know yo' ass. You want her," he said as his gaze went to the door.

A big smile spread on his face and I turned to see Nelly making her way inside. Glancing down at her feet, I noticed she was wearing flat, ballet-looking shoes, but she looked to be in pain. Aaron didn't seem to notice her discomfort. She smiled big and he said, "You know it's on tonight, huh?"

She chuckled and said, "Hell yeah. When East told me you would be here, I knew that I was gonna have to check yo' loud ass."

He chuckled, then hugged her as I watched her. When she turned to me, I could see the weariness in her eyes. "Hey, Nelly."

"Hey, East," she said, then came to my outstretched arms.

I held her tightly for a moment, then kissed her cheek. Before any more words could be said, the hostess led us to a table. I noticed she was moving slowly, and I remembered from our conversation that she'd said when she was stressed, it made the pain worse. "Man, why you moving like a snail? Come get these jokes," Aaron said as I grabbed her hand.

She shook her head as she glanced up at me. While we hadn't been around one another for a long time, she knew what I was asking without me opening my mouth. She was telling me not to tell Aaron what she was going through. I held her hand until she sat, then I scooted into the booth next to her. "So, what'chu been up to, nigga?"

Aaron laughed and said, "I swear you ain't changed. That old age gettin' to you, though, huh? My grandma move faster than you."

That shit was rubbing me the wrong way. I knew he didn't know about her condition, but still. I wanted to interrupt him and tell him to shut the fuck up. Nelly squeezed my thigh as she laughed. "Fuck you, nigga. That old age gettin' to yo' ass, too. That's why them teeth spreading apart? You gon' need dentures before long."

I smiled at her ability to bounce back, but none of this shit was funny to me. Grabbing her hand, I was glad we were sitting in a booth. Intertwining my fingers between hers, I listened to them go back and forth a couple of times, then Aaron laugh and say, "I missed yo' ass, Nel. Where you been?"

"After college, I came back to Houston. I lived there for a couple of years, then we moved back to Beaumont. So, I've been here for damn near fifteen years."

"You must not go many places. You didn't come to the reunions, either."

"Naw. I'm a homebody. I work from home and take care of my family."

"That's cool if that's your thing. I like to get out. Staying in the house all the time would kill my ass."

We laughed as the waitress came and took our drink orders and Nelly released my hand to look at the menu to order some wings.

Once she did, she grabbed my hand again. "So, you had a long day, East?" she asked me.

"Yeah, it was super busy. I literally came straight from work. So, I needed this drink."

"You have to work tomorrow?"

"Yep. Ten to seven."

"They tryna kill you?"

I chuckled. "Well, there are days when it's slow and I get paid to sit there and play on my phone."

I noticed Aaron was silently watching our interaction with a smirk on his lips. I glanced at him, then scooted closer to Nelly to make him think I was gonna talk about him. Leaning over to her ear, I could feel the heat radiating from her. "Why are you wearing shoes? Fuck what people think."

She looked at me, then looked at Aaron and smiled at the frown on his face. She whispered into my ear, "Then Aaron would really clown me and you wouldn't be able to contain yourself."

"Hol' on, na. Y'all ain't finna talk about me like I ain't here."

"We know you're here, Aaron. That's why we're whispering," Nelly said as the waitress brought her two shots and a mixed drink.

I knew that alcohol couldn't be good with all that she had going on, but I couldn't say anything. Aaron laughed and said, "You gon' be fucked up when we leave. You ain't gon' be able to drive."

"Mind yo' business, Aaron," she said as she downed her shots one behind the other.

Aaron lifted his eyebrows as he stared at me. I rolled my eyes and took a swig of my beer. When the waitress came back with Nelly's wings, she did a little dance in her seat and I ordered some Crown. I needed something stronger. When Aaron crossed his legs underneath the table, he must have kicked Nelly. She practically doubled over and said, "Shit!"

"You okay?" I asked.

"My bad, Nelly. I didn't think I kicked you that hard. It was an accident, though. I apologize. Them bones getting fragile."

That was enough. I was done with the jokes. "She has neuropathy in her feet, man. So, chill out."

She swiped the braids from her face and took deep breaths, then glared at me. "I'm sorry, Nelly. Why didn't you say something? I wouldn't have been cracking jokes. My mama have that shit, so I know you in pain," Aaron said.

Her eyes never left mine, and she said, "Had I wanted you to know, I would have told you."

CHAPTER 5

N elsondra

"NELLY, YOU CAN'T BE MAD AT ME ABOUT THAT."

I didn't respond to East. I hated for people to feel sorry for me, and that was just how Aaron was looking at me now. Remaining quiet, I ate my wings as he turned his attention back to his drink and resumed conversation with Aaron. My mood was shit when I got here. Me and Broderick had gotten into it again. This time, he accused me of cheating with East. He had the audacity to say, *No wonder you always tired and your feet always hurting. You probably giving all your energy to that nigga.*

So, since he wanted to accuse me of cheating, I would give him something to be right about. Not that I had any intentions of cheating, but I was almost sure someone he knew would see me out with two men. He could kiss my ass. When he left for work, I left, too. Not only was I angry, but I was hurt even more so. Why would I speak to a man that I was cheating with in front of my family? What would have been the purpose of that? *Jackass.*

So, because of his insistence on me cheating, I told him to go fuck himself and that I was going to leave his ass. He hadn't been gone an hour before he was calling and sending text messages, apologizing. I was so outdone with him. I packed the girls an overnight bag and asked my parents to watch them.

As I sat there quietly eating my wings, I ordered another drink. I was already tipsy, but I just wanted to be at a point where I could forget about my troubles, at least for one night. I hadn't drunk this much alcohol in one sitting in years. I could see East watching me as I ate my wings, waiting for a response. "I'm good, East. Eat some of these wings."

He continued to stare at me as he reached over and grabbed one. "If you think I feel sorry for you, Nelly, guess again. However, I would have been more careful about stretching out my legs, so I wouldn't have kicked you," Aaron said.

"Good."

They resumed their conversation, watching women that were dancing to the music from the live band as the waitress delivered me another shot of Cîroc. Seeing East's eyes grace the curves of other women irritated me. *Why? Bitch, you're married!* That realization still didn't stop me from getting irritated. I wiped my hands and laid a fifty-dollar-bill on the table, then took my shot. "I'm gonna go fellas. Y'all enjoy the rest of your night. You'll let me out, East?"

"Why you leaving? You can't drive."

I crossed my arms over my chest. "Well, if I can't leave or drive, I might as well have another drink."

East scooted closer to me and asked, "What pain are you trying to numb, Nelly? What happened?"

"Nothing. Just get our waitress to bring me another shot of Cîroc."

He rolled his eyes and stopped the waitress as she passed by. I could feel my body relaxing and I knew this next drink would bring me over the edge. When she came back with it, I downed it, then leaned against East. Aaron was laughing, but I didn't care. I felt good as hell. When he looked over at me, I stared into his eyes. East was so damn fine. That beard against his vanilla latte colored skin was doing some things to me it shouldn't have been. He'd also shaved off the gray hairs in his beard, just making him look like a finer version of himself from high school.

The waves in his hair made me seasick and his toned thickness was everything. He was built like a damn defensive back on a football team. The exact position he played in school. He looked powerful, strong, and glancing down at his crotch, well-endowed. East could probably handle a woman my size easily.

I stared at his thick lips, doing my best to resist the urge to kiss them. Whenever I got tipsy, I got horny. I really needed to get home. He kissed my forehead and I closed my eyes briefly. He finished off the wings, then asked the waitress for our tickets. "You ain't gotta leave now, East. Enjoy yourself," I said, hearing my voice slur a little.

"Naw. I gotta work tomorrow. It's time to go."

After the waitress came, East paid our tab and told her to keep the change, then handed me my fifty back. "Save it for next time."

I stuffed it in my shirt as Aaron laughed. "Her ass is lit!"

"Shut up, Aaron," I slurred as I stood.

Yeah. My ass was lit, just as he'd said. I smiled as I stumbled into East. Grabbing my hand, he led me outside, dapped Aaron up, then led me to his car. As he tried to open the door, I fell against the car. He chuckled as I turned around to look at him. He slid his hand over my cheek and asked, "What you running from?"

"Life."

"Well, I need you to find another way to self-soothe."

I pulled him against me and said, "Give me another way."

A drunk man told no lies. This was what I really wanted. I wanted to be free and wanted someone to love me without conditions. His lips crashed into mine and I knew my pussy came alive, feeling new sensations. He pulled away from me just as quickly and he pulled me from against the door, then opened it. I fell into the seat and laughed as he carefully moved my legs inside. He closed the door and I felt like I was floating in my juices.

When he got in, he said, "Listen. That shit can't happen again. What if somebody saw us? You willing to ruin your marriage?"

"My marriage is already ruined."

"Are you leaving him?"

"I don't know."

"Well, until then, you gon' remain faithful."

I was breathing hard, wishing this was a nightmare. Suddenly like a madwoman, I turned to him. "Why can't we just go for what we want? Or is it that you don't want me? This is one-sided. I should've known. No one is ever going to see me past these fucking legs and feet. Let me out," I said, pulling at the door.

"Nelly, keep your drunk ass in this car. You gon' come to my house and I'll bring you back in the morning before I go to work."

"No. I need to be home by seven tomorrow morning. I'll drive."

He rolled his eyes and drove toward my car but didn't stop. He continued to leave the parking lot as I had a fucking fit. "East, this is bullshit! You don't want me! My husband doesn't want me! Let me drive home!"

I pushed his arm to make sure he heard me because he hadn't uttered a word the entire time I was going off on his ass. Finally stopping the car, he turned to me and said, "Shut the fuck up, Nelly. You wanna get fucked? You throwing this fit because you want me to fuck you, so you can go on about your life? Fucking use me to make yourself feel better? Fine. I'll fuck you like a random and send you on your way."

"That's not what I want! I want to feel loved. I wanna be held and made to feel like I'm desirable to some-fucking-body. He already thinks we're fucking anyway. I obviously can't please him, so how in the fuck I'm supposed to please somebody else?"

I brought my hands to my face, feeling like shit as soberness started to creep back in. "I'm sorry. This shit is so fucked up, and I hate that I brought you into my drama and dysfunction. You don't deserve that, East. You're a beautiful soul that will one day be a blessing to a woman who deserves you. It was a mistake going out with you tonight."

I was playing a dangerous game. While East's kiss had nearly melted my damn insides, I couldn't do this like this. This was exactly how people got hurt. I could tell by the way he'd kissed me that he'd *been* wanting to do that. It felt like that shit had been marinating in passion and affection for years. Like he'd been wanting to taste my love since high school. He remained quiet, though. He didn't say anything in response to what I'd said. Within a minute or so, he pulled into the driveway at what I assumed was his house. "East—"

"Shh. Just ride this wave with me. A'ight?"

I nodded my head as he got out of the car. He walked around to my side and opened the door, then helped me out. He held my hand until we got to the door. I stood there, leaning against the house, wondering what was going to happen between us tonight. I didn't have any clothes with me. Tonight wasn't thought all the way through, which proved that this kind of foolishness wasn't typical of me.

Once he got the door open, he grabbed my hand again and led me inside. His home was beautiful. I didn't have time to look around, though, because my feet were killing me. I sat as soon as I could get to the couch and took the flat shoes off. A sigh of relief escaped my lips as East disappeared down a hallway. I laid back against the sofa and closed my eyes. My feet felt like blocks of ice and they were throbbing like crazy. *What were you thinking, Nel?*

As I laid there, I felt him sit next to me. "I can't give you sex. I might turn into a stalker. Knowing how wet that thang get... unless it done changed, I ain't equipped to handle no hot shit like that. But I got something I wanna do for you that I know you'll appreciate. Just trust me, okay?"

I nodded as he stood and helped me to my swollen feet. He glanced down at them and said, "I bet your glucose levels are through the roof. You got your insulin with you?"

"No. But even if I did, I would probably wait until morning to take it, since I didn't eat much. I could bottom out."

I followed him down the hallway to the bathroom where he'd run me a bubble bath. I could have cried. I could count on one hand how many times Broderick had done that for me the entire time we'd been married... fifteen years. He closed the door behind me, then walked to me and gently rubbed my cheek. "You're still so beautiful, Nel."

I could feel my face heat up as I looked away from him. Pulling me closer to him by my waist, he began unbuttoning my top. "I probably shouldn't get in the tub. I won't be able to get out," I said nervously.

"And what the hell am I here for? I can help you, Nel."

"But—"

"But quit talking. I got'chu."

He leaned in and softly kissed my lips, gently pulling my bottom one between his teeth. I was so turned on, but I was scared as hell. When he pulled away, he smiled at me, then pulled my shirt off and unfastened my bra. After staring at me for a moment, he took off my pants and underwear. I was standing there, naked as the day I was born, and I felt so self-conscious suddenly. I wrapped my arms around myself as he shook his head. "Naw, baby. Don't cover this masterpiece."

Leading me to the tub, he helped me in and held me while I sat. I was every bit of two hundred sixty pounds, but he treated me like I was one-ten. The water was hot and relaxing. I released a sigh as he said, "Soak for a lil while. I'll be back in a few minutes."

My eyes scanned his thick frame and I could see the imprint of his erection. I quickly closed my eyes and tried to relax. It was hard to, though. That caramel skin sliding on top of mine was all I could think about. Broderick had been the only man I'd been with for the past twenty years. For me to be fiending for another man like this was foreign to me and I didn't know what to make of it.

When I heard the door close, I opened my eyes and looked around. I was still kind of woozy, but not enough to not be able to take care of myself. *What was I doing here?* Before I could get up to get out of the tub, East came back in the bathroom with a smile. "What'chu doing, Nel? Lay back."

He sat next to the tub. "So why he think we fucking? Why would you have spoken to me if you had something to hide?" Not waiting for me to answer, he said, "I feel like he feels guilty, knowing he isn't everything you need. He thinks you're gonna find everything you need elsewhere. He's insecure in the shit he putting down. Just my opinion."

"You think he's cheating on me?"

"That could be a possibility, too. But I mainly think that he knows he's not making you happy... that he's fucking up."

He grabbed a towel and lathered it up with some Olay body wash. I frowned slightly. "Why do you have Olay body wash?"

He chuckled and that was when I noticed just how gorgeous his smile was. *Damn.* My kitty was gurgling under this water. She was always hot and ready like a damn Little Caesar's pizza. "My mama left it here. We went on a trip a month or so ago and we had to leave early, so she'd spent the night with me. She left it in the shower. No, I ain't tryna walk around smelling all sensitive and shit. Sit up so I can wash you, beautiful."

I smiled softly at him as he began washing me. The tears streamed down my cheeks, but he didn't say a word. He stood to his feet and helped me up, then began washing the rest of my body. He was so gentle when he washed my legs and feet. I was so embarrassed at my rolls and skin discolorations. I'd gained at least seventy pounds since high school. He licked his lips as he stared at my body like it was the most beautiful thing he'd ever seen. "You don't have to look at me like I'm Megan thee Stallion. I know my body is a mess."

"It's a beautiful mess, then. You're gorgeous, Nel."

When he began washing my mound, I could feel my fruit juicing. I spread my legs, giving him access to it as he looked up at me. He again licked his lips as he dragged the towel between my pussy lips. I couldn't help but moan slightly. It felt so sexual and maybe that was because it was. The way he was rubbing me was causing my clit to harden and demand to be sucked. I closed my eyes as he rubbed me, like he was trying to get me to orgasm. Before he could stop, though, my feet were killing me. The position I was in, spreading my legs, caused me to put more pressure on them.

Sensing my discomfort, he stopped and let the water out of the tub, then turned the faucet on. Making sure the temperature was good, he engaged the sprayer and began rinsing me off. The way he was taking care of me had me emotional as hell, wishing I got this at home. He stared into my eyes as he rinsed me, then a smile played at his lips. "Remember when I walked in on you taking a shower?"

I rolled my eyes. "Yeah. I think you did that on purpose."

"I did. That was after I had to fuck Jeremy up. I wanted to see what he was talking about."

I slowly shook my head. "It took you all these years to admit that, huh?"

"Yep. But since you're standing here naked now, I figured I might as well tell the truth. Come on."

I looked around for something to hold onto, but East grabbed me instead. "Hold onto me, Nelly. I got'chu."

My lip was quivering because I hated that he was seeing me this way... weak and dependent. Holding onto him, I carefully lifted my leg to get out as he wrapped his arms around my waist, ensuring that I wouldn't slip. His gesture caused us to be face to face, our lips mere inches apart. I stared at him as he slowly licked his lips. *God, why did he do that?* That tongue looked like it could work magic and every glimpse I got of it, made me wanna say to hell with the pain, I would deal with that later. I needed him.

After helping me out of the tub, East held me close to him, caressing my back. As tall as I was, I still had to look up to him. He was tall as hell... had to be at least six-foot-five, since I was five-ten. I rested my head against his shoulder as he pulled me closer. He kissed my ear, then said, "Come on, Nelly. I'm tryna contain myself, but shit... it's so damn hard."

It sure in the hell was. I could feel his hard dick and it was driving me insane. His hands slid down my back and he grabbed my ass, making the slickness between my legs feel like a pool. Stepping away from me, he grabbed the plush towel from the vanity and dried me off. Just the way he stared at me made me feel loved. *This is what I'm missing.*

I didn't feel loved in my marriage. That was a horrible feeling. Even when I was hurting the most, I managed to cook and wash clothes while working. At least he would have clean clothes to wear and a hot meal to eat when he woke up. I tried cleaning, but I could only stand to do a couple of rooms at a time without getting short-winded.

Here was this gorgeous man, standing in front of me, that only wanted to love me and wanted nothing in return but my love. He knew me better than Broderick ever could, and it was because he took time to talk to me, easing truths out of me that I wouldn't tell a soul otherwise.

CHAPTER 6

E aston

Nelly quietly followed me to my bedroom, but I could feel her tension. "Relax, Nel. Your clothes are in the washing machine, so you'll have something clean to wear in the morning. Let me moisturize your skin. Lay down."

"East, you don't have to do all this. I can put lotion on myself."

"Nelly, lay yo' fine ass down before I give you something that'll have you and those beautiful little girls moving in with me."

She chuckled nervously as she laid in the bed. Why in the fuck was she choosing to stay in an unhappy environment? I couldn't understand it. Just because they had history didn't mean she had to suffer through. But, whatever. I would play whatever role she needed me to play. Taking my shirt off, revealing my tats, I saw her eyes quickly scan me. I pulled off my pants and grabbed the gray sweats from the dresser. After sliding them on, I grabbed the bottle of oil that I used on my skin.

My dick was begging to be free to roam and I knew that she

noticed. Gray sweatpants didn't hide shit, but I wanted to show her that I not only cared about her, but I loved her. I'd been loving Nelly a long time. Now that she was within my grasp, I didn't want to let go. I knew that wasn't up to me. She was married to a jackass. When I turned to her, she looked tense still. "Will you relax? Damn!"

"How can I relax when I'm laying here naked in front of my best friend? Then it looks like you have a fucking hammer in your pants. East, I'm not supposed to be here... I'm not supposed to be feeling you like this. I'm married."

She said that last part softly, like she needed to convince herself of her commitment to her husband. I didn't respond to her. Pouring some oil in my hand, I let it drip on her legs, then began gently rubbing them. "Tell me if I'm applying too much pressure."

"It's perfect," she said as I lifted her leg, getting a glimpse at the soaked treasure between her legs.

Damn! That only made my dick harder. I slowly rubbed her leg as moans slipped from her lips despite her efforts to control them. This shit was a lot harder than I thought it would be. So, instead of focusing on the task, I decided to start conversation. "Tell me why you're here with me. I'm okay with you using me if that's what this is. I know you're married and most likely, you aren't going to leave. So, tell me the role you need me to play in your life. While you were drunk, you wanted me to fuck you, but it seems like you on a different wave right now. Tell me what you want, Nelly."

I gently kissed her foot, then her ankle as she stared at me. She'd always had a special place in my heart, but now that I had experienced life and all that was out there, I realized that I had everything I needed at home. Because of my obsession with the physical attributes of these sack chasers, I missed out on the woman who could have been my forever. "I don't know exactly, East. But I do know I need somebody in my corner to talk to, besides family. I don't like talking about my problems with Broderick to them. If we make up, they'll still be angry, and it would make family moments awkward. I need to feel loved, even if it's not real."

"Nel, I promise you that whatever I make you feel will be real."

I didn't know if I would be able to only be what she said she needed. Seeing her hurt without trying my best to make it better would be hard. I continued to rub her body and listen to her moans. Switching legs, I slowly turned her on her stomach. All that ass was gonna be a distraction as well. Slowly rubbing her other leg, I couldn't help but kiss it as well. Despite her infirmities, Nelly was beautiful. That hadn't changed. What was so hard about that jackass being tender with her?

Once I'd rubbed her leg, I went to her foot and she flinched. "I'm sorry."

"It's okay. My left foot tends to hurt more than my right one, especially my toes."

"Okay, baby girl."

I gently kissed her toes, then barely grazed my fingers over them. Massaging her heel, she moaned, then she started crying... audibly. "Nelly—"

"Please don't stop, East," she got out through her cries.

Rubbing the backs of her legs, I made my way to her ass and massaged it, then worked my way up her back to her shoulders. Her muscles were so tight. She probably needed to see a masseuse or a chiropractor, and I'd be glad to send her to one. As I massaged her neck, her cries got louder. I got in bed with her and pulled her in my arms, letting her cry into my chest. Closing my eyes, I thought about what we were doing. She was wanting me to be her side nigga.

I could play my position, but this was gonna get dangerous. If I didn't have feelings for her, it would be different. I wouldn't engage in these types of activities... period. Married women were off-limits, but Nelly... she wasn't just a married woman. She was my friend and the woman I'd secretly wanted for years. Whatever she wanted from me was hers. Lifting her head, I kissed her tenderly as she lifted her hands to my chest. I thought she was pushing me away, but when she pinched my nipple, I went to the next level.

Separating my lips from hers, I stared at her for a moment. Tilting my head, I tried to read her. Besides her being horny, I didn't know what to think. I rubbed my fingertips over her cheek and said, "Nelly, I'm willing to give you whatever you want. I'm feeling you something serious and I just want to offer you a remedy, physically and emotionally."

"I need you, East," she whispered.

That was all I needed to hear. Lowering my head, I pulled her nipple into my mouth and sucked it, being careful not to apply too much suction. I wanted her to feel passion, desire, and admiration. My hands slowly caressed her body. Her moans were sensual, and they only propelled me forward. Easing my body over hers, I stared into her eyes, then allowed my forehead and nose to rest against hers. I'd never wanted something or someone as badly as I wanted Nelly in this moment. When I saw her on Facebook, I never thought this would be what we were doing almost two weeks later, especially since she was married.

I felt her legs move to my sides, so I asked, "You okay? I'm not hurting you, am I?"

She wrapped her legs around my waist, then pulled my face to hers and kissed me. The heat I felt coming from that kitty, let me know that thang had aged like a fine wine. When Jeremy said her pussy sucked a nigga in, I was angry to hear him speak that way about Nelly, but at the same time, I wanted to know firsthand. She and Jeremy had dated for a few months and when she finally gave it up to him, he couldn't keep his mouth closed. The locker room was filled with stories about Nelly's sexual prowess and how hot her pussy was. I nearly went into a blind rage that day.

Grinding my hips into her, she moaned, then released my lips. "Eeeaast... please take me. Please..."

I closed my eyes briefly, knowing that once I dipped inside of her, there would be no turning back. "Nelly, you sure this what you want? I don't want you to regret this, baby. I'm here whenever you need me. No need to rush into something you aren't sure you're ready for."

She broke down as she let her legs slide back to the bed. I knew she wasn't ready. Sliding to the side of her, I pulled her to me again. "Talk to him honestly, Nelly. Tell him everything you're feeling... like you tell me. If he can't see how you're feeling, then, maybe we can revisit this. Okay?"

"Okay."

"Relax. I'm gonna go put your clothes in the dryer."

I left her in the bed, grabbed the t-shirt from the dresser, and handed it to her. Pulling the comforter over her legs, I said, "I'll be right back."

My dick was cussing me the fuck out, but I wanted to be sure Nelly was ready. She'd had quite a bit of liquid encouragement, causing her to lose sight of what was important... her relationship... her marriage. She needed to close that door. We'd already partially opened a door without her doing so. After putting her clothes in the dryer and I returned to the room, I found that she was asleep that quickly. So, I decided to take a shower. It was getting late, practically one in the morning and she wanted to be home early.

After hopping in the shower, I quickly washed up and washed my beard. It wasn't as long as it was, since I'd gotten a haircut and trim. Those gray hairs had to go. There were only a few, but I'd sport them when they fully took over. When I finished, I walked out to the room and I moisturized with the same oil. I realized that I should have done that in the restroom because Nelly woke up and saw me in all my glory. My dick was hanging and slanging when I walked. It was like she was mesmerized by it. Getting a condom from the drawer, I strapped up. Closing my eyes, I said, "I feel like I can't breathe, Nelly."

"Then come get this oxygen."

Opening my eyes, I joined her in the bed, sliding on top of her. I kissed her lips, then her neck, taking my time with her. After placing kisses on every inch of her skin, I found myself between her legs. Sniffing deeply, I indulged. Rubbing my nose against her clit, I slurped the juice from her fruit and realized it tasted better than I'd ever imagined. Knowing that her legs hurt her, I gently lifted one and rested it on my shoulder so I could get at her better. "Am I hurting your legs, Nelly?"

"No. They feel amazing actually."

The rub down had helped. I was happy about that. Going back to my task at hand, I made love to her with my stiffened tongue, then made my way to her clit. After swirling circles around it with my tongue, I gently sucked it. Simultaneously, Nel sucked in air, then began panting. I could feel the tremble in her legs, but it seemed her orgasm was struggling to show itself. Sliding two of my fingers inside of her and curling them upward, I rubbed circles on her g-spot, while continuing to suck her clit. When her weaker leg lifted in the air, I knew I had her. "Eeeaaassst! Shiiiit!"

She came so hard and I continued to give her everything she needed, slurping that shit up as quickly as I could. Hearing her scream my name, though... fuck! Withdrawing my fingers, I knew my dick had to be up in there. Making sure the condom was good, I slowly pushed inside of her and her eyes opened. I bit my bottom lip, knowing that Jeremy was right as hell over twenty years ago. Her shit was hot, gushy, and powerful. "Oh, fuck, Nel."

I was caught off-guard with just how good it was. She arched her back as she continued to stare at me. Digging her nails in my shoulder, she said, "Oh my God, East. You feel so fucking good. Fuck!"

I began stroking her roughly and she loved every minute of it. My grunts and her screams of passion were getting to me. I needed to be in her pussy for as long as possible, because I had a feeling it would be a while before I felt it again, if at all. Pulling away from her, I rolled her over to her knees. "This position good for you, baby?"

"Yeah. It's my preferred position."

Pulling her up by her hips, I dipped back into the kamikaze of perfection. This shit was deadly, reckless, and foolish, but it was perfect at the same damn time. Gripping her ass, I long stroked her pussy, watching the juices coat every inch of me. I could feel her juices leaking to my balls and at that moment I wanted to live inside of her hot tavern forever. I was drunk with perfection and it seemed like she'd put some kind of spell on me. She'd never expressed interest in voodoo, but her pussy was an expert at it... a damn witch doctor, healing me from the inside out.

I needed to fuck her. "Nelly, can I straddle your legs?"

"Yeah."

I did just that as my dick rested inside of her, pulsating, waiting to get back to action. She lifted her hips, tooting her ass up and I pushed into her, feeling like I dove into everlasting love. It was so damn intense; I couldn't control the trembles that coursed through my body. The goosebumps that appeared on my skin came from nowhere and I couldn't help but growl as I dug out her pussy. "Fuck, Nelly! Your shit is so good, baby. I'm about to nut."

"Give it to me, East. Fuck me up... please, baby."

I dug into her shit like it would be my last time to experience sex, feeling her end and her walls tighten around me. "East! I'm cumming! Oh... shit!"

When her walls gripped me, I had to give up the ghost. My dick was like, *who is this pussy?* I shot off into the latex and I nearly collapsed on top of her. "Damn, Nel. Shit."

When I rolled off her, I had to lay on my back and find my fucking self. It felt like I'd been catapulted out of this world. She snuggled into my arms and I kissed her head, wishing that things were different and that I wouldn't have just committed suicide.

CHAPTER 7

N elsondra

"I JUST WANT THINGS TO GO BACK TO THE WAY THEY WERE. IT feels like our marriage is spiraling out of control. How do we stop it? I love you, Nelly. I want us to work."

Whenever we talked, my feet throbbed like they were being cut off. I was tired of trying to make us work. It didn't help that I was missing East. I couldn't believe we'd had sex. Whenever I thought about it, I cried. Not because I regretted it, but because it was the most passionate sex I'd ever had. *I'm married, though. Shouldn't my husband make me feel those things?* Easton had made my body feel like it had never felt before... like I was a virgin, touched for the very first time. The rub down beforehand had my legs feeling brand new and my feet weren't hurting as bad. But that was almost two weeks ago.

When I'd gotten home that next morning, I'd hurriedly taken another shower, hating that I had to wash the oil off that East had rubbed me down with. I had to get his scent off me. I cried the entire time I was in the shower. Now that I'd had him... felt him inside of me... I wanted more. Being caught was my biggest fear. But it was like East knew I was gonna disappear for a minute when he dropped me off. He'd said, *Don't go ghost on me.* But that was exactly what I'd done.

Then once Broderick got home that morning, we'd had a huge fight. He wanted to question me about where I'd been. Because of modern technology, he could tell where my car was through an app on his phone. I'd forgotten all about that, so I was glad I didn't drive to Easton's house. Getting him caught up in drama wasn't my intent, so I would die if that happened. That was why I had to do something about my relationship... my marriage to Broderick. "I'm tired. I really am."

Today, we'd gotten into it because I'd turned him down for sex. When I did, he went into the kitchen and cooked enough food for himself, then went to bed. For some reason, he didn't see anything wrong with that. I was beyond pissed that he could be so selfish. "What are you saying Nelly? You want me to leave? You want a divorce?"

"I'm really trying, but I feel like I'm fighting a losing battle. It seems like you can't see past yourself and I don't know what else to do. It feels like you aren't even trying. I don't feel loved. You saying it doesn't mean a damn thing if I don't feel it. Ever since I was diagnosed with neuropathy, I can't seem to please you anymore. That hurts. Where are the vows we took? In sickness and in health? That was obviously a joke to you."

"It's been a huge adjustment and I'm trying! I can't believe you want to leave me over that."

"That's the fucking problem! You don't take this seriously! I'm fucking tired of feeling like I'm not enough for you! I hate feeling like all this is my fault! The weight of this marriage is heavy as hell and I'm fucking drained! Why can't you see how much this hurts? Are you still in love with me?"

"Yeah, but how can I be excited about working all night, then having to come home and take care of you?"

It felt like I had been stabbed in the heart. "Take care of me? What the fuck do you do to take care of me? You haven't done anything that you haven't been doing for our entire marriage. The adjustment was that I can't move around as much during sex."

And now that I'd had sex with East, it seemed like sex with Broderick was mediocre. I'd never had an orgasm during sex until I'd been with East. The shit snuck up on me and I was shocked as hell that it had happened. He took the time to learn every curve my insides took and paid attention to my reactions when he hit certain spots. The way he caused my body to react to his touch... his stroke... the shit was unbelievable. "Nelly, that's not true! Sometimes, I cook."

"Again! That was shit you were doing before my diagnosis!"

I took deep breaths and realized that this was repetitive and unhealthy. It was damn near toxic. Standing from the bed, I literally fell to the floor because my feet were hurting that badly. He reached his hand out to me to help, but I screamed for him to get away from me. "See, I'm tryna help yo' ass now, but you too stubborn to accept it!"

He pulled me up as I fought him. I didn't want him even touching me at this point. He was too stupid to even realize that it was because of him that my feet were hurting worse. Whenever I got stressed out, my glucose levels, blood pressure... everything went through the fucking roof. I laid in the bed, refusing to look at him. Then I decided to just get out of the house. I didn't care how badly I was hurting. *Call East.* "Girls, get dressed!" I yelled from my bedroom.

I knew they were hearing our arguments. And I was almost sure they would ask me about it. "Where the hell y'all going?"

"Mind our fucking business. If you're going to work, go to fucking work!"

He huffed loudly, then threw a bottle water across the room, knocking one of my picture frames to the floor. It happened to be our engagement picture. *Perfect.* I slid into my blue jeans, put some socks on, then slid on my house shoes. I needed some new ones. These were so comfortable, but I couldn't find the same type of shoe anywhere. I didn't really shop for myself anyhow. Everything I did was for my children and Broderick. When he walked out of the room, I could hear him telling the girls bye and kissing them.

I huffed loudly and grabbed my phone and purse. When I came out of the room, looking a God-awful mess, I supposed that was good enough for him. Had I combed my hair and put on makeup, he would have been alarmed, even though I had our daughters with me. He was so insecure, when I felt like I was the one to have a reason to be. But thinking about how much I enjoyed sex with East, I guess he did have a reason to be insecure. "Mommy, where are we going?"

"I thought y'all might wanna go to get ice cream."

"Yay! Thanks, Mommy!"

They were beyond happy. I watched them both grab their purses and we headed out the door to see their dad backing out of the driveway. They excitedly waved at him and he blew the horn as he drove away. It would kill them if we left him. I was suffering for their happiness. Once we were in the car, just as I thought, Zahria asked, "Mommy, why were you and Daddy arguing?"

"It's nothing for the two of you to worry your pretty little heads about. Okay? It's something your dad and I have to work through."

"Okay," they said in unison.

We continued to Marble Slab Creamery. When we got there, I saw a familiar car. It looked a lot like East's car, but there were a ton of Impala's around Beaumont. Making our way inside, I was almost paralyzed when I saw him sitting there with a woman. She'd fed him a spoon of frozen yogurt. Doing my best to pick my heart up before I tripped over it, I headed to the counter. He noticed me as we walked by, but he didn't acknowledge me. This was hard and it was all my fault. The girls ordered what they wanted while I stood there, wishing that I'd stayed home. "Ma'am?"

I assumed I had zoned out because the girls giggled. "I'm sorry. Yes, ma'am?"

"Will there be anything else?"

"No, ma'am."

"Mommy, you aren't getting any?"

"No. I just wanted the two of you to have some."

I glanced over at East to see him watching me. After paying for their desserts, I was heading out when he said, "Hey, Nelly."

Turning to him, I said softly, "Hey, East."

I could feel the lump in my throat and the tears threatening to cascade down my cheeks. The girls were so into their frozen yogurt, what I'd convinced them was ice cream, they didn't see or hear a thing until East said, "Hey, girls. How are y'all?"

The woman he was with was impatiently looking on, like me and my kids were threatening to take him away from her. The girls smiled and waved, then Tiana said, "Oh, I remember you! You're Mommy's friend from school."

"Yep," he said, glancing up at me.

"Okay, girls, let's go."

I had to get out of there. My chest was pounding as my heart sat between my feet. "See you around, Nelly."

I nodded and quickly left, getting to the car so fast, I was out of breath. When I eased into the driver's seat, my feet were tingling, and my toes had shooting pains going through them. Turning the music up after starting the car, I cried. I'd created a mess. Leaning my head on the steering wheel, I tried to compose myself as I felt a tap on my shoulder. Lowering the volume, I said, "Yes, baby?"

"Your friend is at the window, Mommy," Zahria said.

"Can you put on 'Savage'?" Tiana asked.

I found the edited version of the song, then lowered my window. Wiping the tears from my eyes, I looked up at him. "You okay?" he asked.

I shook my head, then said, "But I'll be fine. Go enjoy your date."

He stood there watching me, sympathy and love in his eyes... love for his friend that he'd made feel like more. Like he'd said that night, he felt like he couldn't breathe, I felt the same way. I lifted my window, then backed out of my parking spot, leaving him standing there watching us leave. As I drove home, I got an incoming call from Broderick. I didn't want to answer it, but I knew he would keep calling until I did. "Yes?"

"I love you, Nelly. I'm sorry. Please don't leave me."

"I have to go, Broderick. I can't do this right now."

"Just tell me this. Do you still love me?"

"Yeah. That's why this is so devastating. I don't feel like you love me anymore."

I ended the call because I couldn't control my cries. Looking in my rearview mirror, I saw my babies watching me. They'd begun to cry, too, and that hurt my heart. "Mommy's okay, babies. Y'all stop crying."

I wasn't too convincing, being that I was crying while I said it. Once we turned in the driveway, I got out of the car as quickly as possible. I just wanted to take my Lyrica and go to bed. When I unlocked the door, I opened it so the girls could walk through first. The way I was walking, I felt like an old woman, hunched over and hobbling. I took my meds, then said, "Don't stay up too late girls. I'm going to bed. My feet are killing me."

"Okay, Mommy. I'll come check on you when I finish my ice cream."

"Okay, baby."

Tiana was the one who thought she was the mommy when I wasn't around or when I was feeling bad. Zahria hugged me, then said, "I love you, Mommy."

"Love you, too, suga plum."

I made my way to my room as my phone rang again. It was Broderick and I just couldn't. My emotions were already all over the place and I didn't wanna make it worse. When I got to my room, I fell onto the bed, then pulled my blanket over me.

⚜

"Mmm, I love you, Nel. Damn, baby."

I woke up to Broderick's fucking fingers in my pussy, stroking me. Per usual, she was wet as hell. It felt like I was getting some of the best sleep of my life and to wake up to this was irritating as hell. Last night, nothing had been resolved, no conclusion had been reached. Why in the hell did he feel this was okay? *Because of you, Nel.* I always gave in and let him have his way. I was dying inside, though.

He rolled me over and slid my pants and underwear off, not bothering to ask me how I was feeling or if I was in any pain. My legs were always stiffer in the mornings. I was at my worst in the mornings. Everything hurt. He knew that. But only his needs mattered. It had been that way our entire marriage. I'd never had an orgasm during sex with him and instead of him trying to find ways to make me cum, he accepted that something was wrong with me, since I didn't cum. *East made me cum, though.* That shit was so mind-blowing, I couldn't stop thinking about it.

Broderick and I had had one enjoyable day last week. I was feeling pretty good and we'd had sex three times that day, but the past week we'd been at odds once again and I'd been feeling like shit. He grabbed my legs by the back of my knees, pushing them up. I winced in pain as he slid his dick inside of me, humping me fast. "Damn. That pussy always ready for daddy, huh?"

I didn't respond, just kept my eyes closed. Feeling the urge to cry, I quickly swallowed that shit. Crying over him and his selfish ways solved nothing. As if tired of looking at my face, he roughly turned me over by throwing my leg to the bed, then swiftly entered me again, pulling my hips to him, forcing me on my knees. He fucked me hard and slapped my ass as he growled. "Shit, Nel, I'm about to nut," he whispered in my ear.

He'd straddled one leg and pushed the other up as far as it would go. Although he didn't have all his weight on my leg, just the pressure of him being on it had it numb. My entire left leg was tingling. It was the worst of the two. He fucked me until he satisfied himself, thrusting himself inside of me, splitting my pussy. He always did that shit. I assumed because he was a big nigga, his stomach got in the way and he tended to enter me at awkward angles that my pussy hated. I could feel it stinging.

He rolled off me, then went to the bathroom to get a towel. I felt so emotionless, but this was the life I'd created for myself. This was what I'd accepted over the years. When he came back with the towel, he said, "You must have gon' to bed horny. You was wet, wet."

Taking the towel from him, I wiped myself, then went to the bathroom to brush my teeth. I still had yet to say a word to him. Limping my way to the bathroom, I heard him say, "Girl, you limping in there like an old woman. I thought I stretched all those limbs out."

I was starting to hate him.

Why couldn't I leave? The girls would adjust to whatever decisions I made for us. Something wasn't right, though. I smelled cologne. Broderick never wore cologne to work. Seemed like I wasn't the only one to step outside of our marriage. He was seeing someone else and for some reason, that made me smile.

CHAPTER 8

E aston

"Are you gonna get off on time today?"

"It seems I will. We haven't been terribly busy. I'll call you closer to ending time. You wanted to kick it?"

"Yeah, maybe go to dinner."

"A'ight. I'll call you later."

I ended the call with Whitney, a woman I'd been talking to for the past month or so. Just as I figured, Nelly had ghosted me. When I saw her in Marble Slab almost three weeks ago, I could tell she was going through the same bullshit and she looked ten years older than the night when she was in my bed. Part of me felt sorry for her and the other part of me was angry with her. I wanted her to wake up and see that he was dragging her through the mud. That couldn't be healthy for her or her girls.

Making love to her felt like heaven and to have it taken away from me made me feel like I was living in hell. It was taking everything in me to resist messaging her, especially after seeing her in

Marble Slab. It was like her soul was crying for me to save her. I wanted to save her, show her that I could love her through all her pain. But I could only do what she allowed me to do... which wasn't a damn thing.

I met Whitney at work. She was there buying a car and she caught my attention when I heard her laugh. Truthfully, she sounded a lot like Nel. While they looked nothing alike, over the phone it sounded like I was talking to her. One time, I'd almost called her Nelly. I was talking to her, but I really didn't feel a thing between us. I hadn't even made a move to initiate sex with her, despite the hints she was throwing out there. I felt like I'd settled for the next best thing.

As I waited for funding for a customer, I opened up messenger, just to scroll through our conversation. Why did I have to have sex with her? Her soul had tied itself to mine and it wouldn't let go for shit. It was almost like some August Alsina, Jada Pinkett shit. The only difference was that I wasn't mentally unstable, and she wasn't who she was pretending to be, either. She wasn't as strong as she often tried to pretend to be. I knew her well and the only time she hid from me was when she was feeling weak. Not only that, but she was an extremely loyal person, so having sex with me was out of character for her.

When I saw the dots appear like she was typing, I got excited, but then they disappeared. Taking a deep breath, just as I was about to close out of the app, a message came through. *I'm sorry. It probably means nothing to you at this point, but I am. I got involved emotionally and physically at a time when I wasn't available. I thought I would be available two weeks ago, but then I ended up in the hospital for a stupid boil. I'm back home, but I'm not totally better. I just wanted you to know that I was thinking of you and I missed you.*

I rubbed my hand down my face and began typing out my response as my heart felt heavy for her. *I miss you, too, and I hate waiting for you to reach out. I'm a grown-ass man. You don't have to apologize for shit. I knew what I was getting into when I slid in that sweet pussy. I need to see you, Nelly. So, whenever you can, Facetime me or video call me through messenger.*

Sending the message, I sat my phone on the desk and noticed that an approval had come through, but the interest rate was high. When Mr. Jeffcoat came back from the restroom and sat in front of me, I said, "Only one has come in so far. The interest rate is twelve percent, though. With your credit score, we should be able to get a better rate. I'm just waiting on more approvals to come through."

"Okay. Is it cool if I get my daughter to pick me up and come back to wrap up the paperwork?"

"Sure. No problem. I'll call you when we're ready for you to sign."

"Okay, thanks, Easton."

We shook hands and he headed out. He'd come through my office to finance a car before, so we were familiar. He called me Mr. Bridges at first, but I insisted that he called me Easton. I needed him to feel comfortable if I wanted to drive that sell home, adding warranties to it. Selling warranties lined my pockets nicely, so I tried to do that with every customer. I didn't sell them no wolf tickets, though, because that could bite me in the ass. I explained the benefits of the warranty and left the decision up to the customer.

When he walked out, I went back to my phone to see Nelly had responded. *I can't call until tonight. He went to the store to get me some crackers. I've been extremely nauseated and whenever I eat food, I can't keep it down. So, I had a few minutes of alone time.*

Just knowing that she'd been in the hospital only increased my need for her. Nel didn't like sympathy, but if I could hold her in my arms, I would feel so much better. *Shit.* I had a date tonight. She couldn't call because I wouldn't be available. Before I could respond, she sent, *I'm sorry. I know you have someone now. If you're available, message me. He works nights. I have to go.*

Why was I putting myself through this? *Because you love her ass.* I was supposed to be the man to offer her love unmatched, care unfathomable, and safety from life's turmoil. For a while, my mind wanted me to think that she just used me, and I was cool with that, too, but I thought better of it. Nelly wasn't the type. I could see that she wasn't happy when I saw them together at McAlister's before she even noticed I was there. The way he left her at the table when it was time for them to go let me know that he was a jackass.

The pop-up box on my computer screen brought my attention back to the present. Mr. Jeffcoat had another approval for ten percent. Shaking my head slowly, I tried to busy myself getting the previous deal I'd done together, so I could bring it to accounting. But that task didn't keep my mind off Nelly. I almost wanted to cancel with Whitney just so I could talk to her. She seemed so fragile. If I knew where she lived, I'd scoop her and her little dolls up, taking them away from a nigga that seemed preoccupied with other things.

I couldn't speak on what kind of father he was, but if Nelly wasn't happy, I knew they'd noticed. My mind was consumed with her even before we'd had sex. That night, though, replayed through my mind repeatedly. Sex with her just wasn't sex. We had an emotional connection. The shit felt spiritual. There was so much more to it than I ever imagined there would be. The passion between us was something I'd never felt in my forty years... almost forty-one years on this earth.

It was like my heart spoke in whispers to my soul. *Nelly... Nelly... Nelly.* That was all it said, but even with just saying her name, it was saying a lot. Standing from my desk, I decided to go get a Snickers. Although I had eaten lunch, I just felt famished. As I walked around the corner, my phone rang. Grabbing it from my pocket, I saw it was my mama. I answered, "What's up, Ma?"

"Hey, baby boy. You gotta work the weekend?"

"No ma'am. I'm off this Saturday."

"Perfect! I'm giving you a birthday dinner and I don't wanna hear shit about you don't want a celebration. Just be here Saturday at four."

"Ma—"

"What I say, boy?"

"A'ight. Just no funny business."

"Whatever. Get back to work."

She ended the call as I shook my head slowly. She was always trying to hook me up with somebody. My birthday was Monday coming up, but I had no intentions of celebrating. I thought briefly about inviting Whitney, but my mama would embarrass me. She could always sniff out bullshit. And she would straight up tell

Whitney that she was wasting time with me. *Maybe I should bring her.* I was tired of pretending with Whitney. I could tell she was feeling me and wanted more, but I couldn't give her that. I was in love with Nelly.

Being in love with Nelly was probably why I hadn't had a meaningful relationship, well besides my engagement. But even then, I wasn't really sold on being anybody's husband. Subconsciously, I'd been wanting Nelly for years. That was what I believed. I'd been in love with her for a long time, but I finally realized it when I saw her again. I was willing to bet my mama was gonna invite Nelly through Facebook. Grabbing my Snickers, I headed back to my desk to get this day done and have an unfulfilling dinner with Whitney.

JUST LIKE I FUCKING THOUGHT...

If I didn't know my mama, then my name wasn't Easton Bridges. When Whitney and I walked in, she gave her the once over and I could see some shit was 'bout to fly out of her mouth. I quickly pulled Whitney away from her and we sat on the couch with Aaron and a couple of my boys from school. We were catching up while Whitney sat quietly, until my mama asked, "How long y'all been together?"

"We aren't really together. We're just getting to know each other. But it's been a little over a month now," Whitney responded.

"Hmm. If Easton was really feeling you, baby, you would be his already. Stop wasting your time with somebody who ain't gon' move past this phase y'all in."

I lowered my head. Mama never disappointed. She always did my dirty work for me. We hadn't been here an hour yet and she'd already destroyed Whitney's hopes and dreams. Somebody broke her filter years ago and she ain't been able to find one that fit since then. Whitney cleared her throat and crossed her legs glancing at me, probably expecting me to say something. There was nothing for me to say, other than, "Ma, chill out."

She frowned and before she could respond, the doorbell rang.

After rolling her eyes at me, she went to it. Whitney immediately turned to me and asked, "Is that true? You not feeling me?"

Aaron snickered as I said, "I really like you, Whitney. But I'm not really feeling a connection between the two of us. You're cool to go out with, but I'm not seeing us pursuing anything else beyond that."

"And you couldn't tell me that?"

"I was trying to give it more time."

When mama walked back in holding some woman's hand, I knew this was going to be a long evening. The lady glanced at me and blushed as Mama introduced her. "Easton this is Brandi. She goes to church with me."

"Of course she does," I said under my breath. "Hello, Brandi. Nice to meet you."

"Likewise, Easton. Happy birthday."

"Thank you."

When the doorbell rang again, Mama took off for the door. I heard her scream in excitement, then say, "I didn't think you were going to make it! Easton is going to be so surprised."

I frowned immediately, knowing my mama was really on some bullshit. Nobody knew how to stir the pot like her. And again, just as I thought, Nelly and her daughters entered the room.

CHAPTER 9

N elsondra

WHEN MS. ALICE MESSAGED ABOUT EAST'S BIRTHDAY DINNER, I was feeling so bad. I'd told her that I would be there if I was feeling better. I couldn't miss East's birthday. I wasn't feeling one hundred percent, but I needed to get out of the house and away from Broderick's ass. He was suffocating the fuck out of me. He'd taken off work a couple of days to supposedly take care of me, but I was still having to cook and clean until my mama called to see how I was feeling. She came right over, hearing in my voice that I felt horrible. It turned out, they had me on an antibiotic that my body didn't agree with and it was keeping me nauseated.

Seeing the shock on East's face made me smile slightly. I'd worn some capri pants and a low-cut round-neck cotton shirt, nothing dressy, but not my normal warm-up pants and t-shirt, either. He stood from his seat and hugged me, then my girls. Tiana handed him the gift bag and Zahria gave him a card. Looking up at me, he said, "Mama's right. I'm surprised."

His gaze had me feeling warm inside, so I looked away, noticing his friend from the ice cream parlor was here. She had that same look on her face that she did that day. I cleared my throat and said, "Well, happy birthday."

The girls repeated my sentiments and East smiled big and said, "Thank you."

I could feel my legs weakening, so I made my way to a chair at the table, away from East and his guests. The girls sat next to me and Ms. Alice joined me. "So how are you feeling? You don't look so good."

"I'm not at my best, but I couldn't miss Easton's birthday."

"If you don't mind me asking, what's wrong?"

I'm in love with a man who doesn't seem to give a damn about me. "I had a boil on my inner thigh. I'd gone to like an urgent care and they drained it. It felt so much better, but by the time the weekend was over, it had gotten bigger. So, I went to the emergency room that Monday and they admitted me. They had to surgically remove it. I was in the hospital for ten days. I got home a week ago, but the antibiotics have been keeping me drained and nauseated."

"Wow. I'm so sorry, baby. Have y'all been taking care of your mama?"

As she talked to the girls, asking their names and ages, I quickly glanced over at East to see him watching me. The past month and a half had been horrible without him. I felt lonely... even with Broderick lying next to me. This morning had been the final straw. As I was sleeping, I felt him easing his fingers in my underwear. I still had a fucking hole in my leg, which happened to be inches away from my glory hole. I slapped his hand away, then got up from the bed, nearly falling on the floor.

I was always at my worst in the mornings, he knew that. Like an old woman, I had to stretch and let my bones crack and get my bearings. As if my legs weren't weak enough, they were always weaker in the mornings. When I nearly fell face-first to the floor, he never even flinched to try to help me. He just lay there in bed, stroking his dick. However, by the time I came out of the restroom, he was up and getting dressed. His exact words were, *"Nelly, I'm sorry, but I don't know how long I can go without."*

My response to him was, *"Why don't you just go do what you've been doing? You've been getting relieved by Tracy anyway."*

He'd stood there in shock. I'd done my research. When he started wearing cologne all the time, I knew something was up. So, I started searching through the phone records. That one number kept popping out at me. There were other numbers on there that I didn't know, but that one gave me bad vibes all the way around. I called it, pretending to be a doctor's office and the stupid bitch gave me her full name, talking about she'd been waiting on a call from SETMA, a local group of medical professionals.

I'd been waiting for an opportunity to throw the shit in his face. Did I feel like a hypocrite? Yes. But at least I was smart enough not to get caught. Our marriage was on its last leg already. We were both disappointed with my inabilities. I felt like I couldn't please him no matter how hard I tried, and he made me feel inadequate for him... like everything was my fault. It was like he thought that I'd prayed for all these health issues to happen to me.

It was in my genes. I'd been diabetic for twenty years, eighteen years when I was diagnosed with neuropathy. I'd had no other issues until two years ago... my first complications from being diabetic and having polycystic ovarian syndrome, which could affect every organ in the body. His empathy for me was nonexistent. Me being here wasn't about East. Although I didn't want to miss his birthday dinner, being here was about me gaining my independence from a man that couldn't see past himself.

Before Broderick left, I told him that I was done. I'd been with-holding the information I knew about him and Tracy until the perfect time. Today, the time was perfect. I told him that he could buy me out and keep the house. He tried to apologize by falling to his knees, crying and begging me not to leave, but my heart was hard. I'd had enough. "Nelly! Bring yo' crazy self over here," Aaron yelled out.

I glanced at East and his woman, not wanting to make a move. The look on her face told me that she knew about East's feelings for me and she felt threatened. Not only that but I had the nerve to feel jealous. *What I wouldn't give to lay in his arms right now.* Ms. Alice had my girls in the kitchen with her and I wasn't sure what they were doing. I'd zoned out thinking about my troubles. "Shut up, Aaron," I said, then headed to the kitchen.

They were helping her fix bowls of gumbo for everybody, so I went to the kitchen to help her. "Nel, you should be out there catching up with everyone else."

"I'm not about to let you do this by yourself."

She smiled at me as I slowly walked to her and grabbed East and his girlfriend's bowls from her. Walking back to the table, I sat their food there and said, "East, you and your lady's food is on the table."

He nodded and smiled at me as he stood and helped her to her feet. Going back to the kitchen, I grabbed two more bowls and brought them out as Tiana and Zahria brought out drinks. Ms. Alice had an eight-chair table, but there wouldn't be enough room for me and the girls once we finished serving everybody. East had six friends in attendance, including his girlfriend, and that extra seat would be for Ms. Alice.

After getting the girls situated on the floor around the coffee table, I went back to the kitchen to get my bowl. It smelled so good and my stomach was growling in response to it. Before I could get to my children, Ms. Alice said, "Sit to the table, baby. I'm gonna sit with the girls. We are getting along just fine."

I smiled at her, then made my way to the table. Besides Easton, his girlfriend and Aaron, there were three other guys and a lady. I wasn't sure who any of them were. When I sat, all eyes seemed to be on me, and I felt extremely uncomfortable. As if sensing that, East said, "Everybody, this is one of my best friends, Nelsondra Garrett."

Surprised that he used my married name, I responded, "Nelsondra Allison. But everybody calls me Nel or Nelly."

His eyebrows lifted slightly, which let me know he was getting my drift. Everyone spoke to me, then continued eating. The gumbo was so good, I wanted to get seconds, but I didn't want to embarrass myself like that. I was already a big girl. I didn't need to bring attention to myself. Broderick had made numerous "jokes" about my weight, including one where he told me I looked like two gallons of milk in my wedding gown. I wasn't that big according to my mama. I wore a size eighteen, but I was pushing a twenty. All during school, I wore a twelve to a fourteen.

Standing from the table, I went to check on my girls and they were done eating and chatting with Ms. Alice. I sat next to her and she said, "Hug me, baby."

I frowned slightly, not knowing why she wanted me to hug her. But I did so, and she whispered in my ear, "You're hurting. I can see it. I can also see how much East loves you. I think you love him, too."

The tears fell from my eyes as I pulled away from her and she nodded. Quickly wiping them before the girls saw, I could see East staring at me once again. *Shit!* I wasn't trying to talk about my issues at his party. So instead of hanging around until the party was over, I cleaned up after the girls and said, "We're going to go."

"Already? We haven't eaten birthday cake yet," Ms. Alice said.

"I shouldn't have that anyway. I'm sorry, Ms. Alice, but we really have to go."

"Mommy, do we have to?" Zahria asked.

"Yes, baby. Mommy isn't feeling too well."

"Aww, okay."

I walked over to East as he stood from his seat and said, "I'll walk y'all out."

I nodded, then said, "Nice meeting all of you. Aaron, go to hell."

Everyone laughed and said the same, then we headed outside. I started the car from the remote and unlocked the doors. As Tiana and Zahria ran to hop in, East grabbed my hand. Turning to face him, he asked, "You left him?"

"I told him today that we were done. Not that I'm any better, but he's fucking someone else, so it's time to let go."

"So, all we did was fuck?" he asked as he stared at me.

Lowering my head for a moment, I looked back up at him as a tear fell from my eye. "No. I could never call what we experienced just a fuck. It was so much more, East... more than I thought it would be."

I'd gotten used to Broderick's mediocrity. There was one speed during sex with him. Fast. It made me feel like he was just trying to hurry it along and get a nut. There were no tender moments to assure me that he gave a fuck about the person attached to the pussy. He didn't care about pleasing me, making a connection with me while experiencing my most intimate parts. East swiped my tear away and said, "I love you, Nelly. I want to see you happy."

I heated up tremendously as I pulled away from him. My daughters were in the car and I couldn't have them feeding Broderick nothing incriminating. He glanced at them, then smiled at me. "Don't be a stranger, Nel. Hit me up whenever. If you need me, you know I'll come running."

I shook my head. "I'm not a homewrecker, East. But I'll message you from time to time."

"She's not my girlfriend, just somebody I was talking to. But umm... Alice got ahold of her. Told her the real."

"Oh Lawd," I said, then laughed.

He laughed, too. I rubbed my hand over his cheek. East was such a gorgeous man. "Get back inside to your guests."

He smiled and opened my door for me. The girls were on the tablets they'd left in the car, not paying the least bit attention to me. After I sat, he leaned over and helped me get my legs in the car. I smiled softly at him and prepared to make my descent to hell when I got home. I knew when I got there, he would be back, ready to get on my fucking nerves. As we sat at a red light, I grabbed the bottle of Lyrica from my purse and popped a pill, drinking water from my thermos that I'd brought with me. "Mommy, are your feet hurting?" Tiana asked.

"Yeah, baby. Did y'all enjoy the party?"

"Ms. Alice was nice. It didn't seem like a party," Zahria said.

I chuckled. "Yeah, that's 'cause it wasn't a kid's party, Z," Tiana said to her.

"I know that, Tiana. I was talking to Mommy."

I shook my head slowly. Tiana thought she had to boss everything. According to my family, she was a lot like me. I wasn't like that at her age, though. I was that way as an adult and before my diagnosis two years ago. I'd changed a lot since then and I'd watched my self-esteem take a nosedive. I hated that I'd allowed neuropathy and Broderick to do that to me. Neuropathy was hard enough, I shouldn't have to fight my spouse, too. As I took a deep breath, my phone chimed. When I stopped, I grabbed it to see a message from East. *Sorry for messaging, but I had to tell you how beautiful you looked. I miss your presence already, Nelly.*

My mind went to East and I was wondering if he meant he loved me or that he was in love with me. We'd always told one another *I love you*, but it felt different this time. If I didn't have the girls with me, I would have kissed him right there. I had to wait until I got to another light to message him back. *Thank you. You always look amazing, East. I miss you, too. But we'll be able to talk more often once we move in with my parents.*

It was funny that I even mentioned moving. I hadn't spoken to my family about any of this. Sitting my phone down, I could hear a horn blaring behind me. The light was green. My phone chimed again, and I was wondering how he was messaging me so much while he entertained his guests. When I drove in the driveway, I turned the notifications off for messenger and read his message. *Okay. Message me when you can.*

I didn't bother responding to him, because I didn't want him to message again. Broderick was indeed home, and the bastard was standing at the door watching us. "Daddy!" the girls yelled.

I rolled my eyes as I struggled to get out of the car. My feet had all types of pain shooting through them just at the sight of him. He hugged the girls, then rushed to my side. The moment he reached out, I jerked away from him. "Why do you wanna help me now? Any other time you'd let me struggle alone."

"Nel, I'm sorry."

"You ought to be sick of saying you're sorry, because frankly, I'm tired of hearing the shit."

I slammed the door of my car and brushed past him, with a renewed sense of energy. Just before I could tell the girls to pack, my phone started ringing. Looking at it to see my daddy's cell phone number, I answered. "Hello?"

"Hey, Nel. What y'all up to?"

"Not too much, Daddy. What about y'all?"

I wanted to tell him what was really going on, but with Broderick standing in my face, my nerves were everywhere. They loved him and thought he was such a great man... and he was, but he was a piss poor husband. He thought about me, sometimes, but it seemed it was only for applause. I didn't feel the sincerity in none of it. Maybe I was the one who changed. I had to admit, I spoiled the hell out of him in our marriage, but now that I needed him... that I was down... he decided to kick me, instead of help me up. "Your sister left her husband. Her and Jonathan are here with all of their clothes."

"Oh no. What happened?"

Well, there went that. The girls and I didn't have anywhere to go, now. I refused to take them out of here to be uncomfortable. Had it just been me, I could have slept in my car. "I don't know exactly. Once she gets situated, we're gonna talk."

"Man, I hate that, but if that's what's best for her and Jonathan, I support her."

"Yeah. You sure you okay?"

"Yes, sir. I'm just a little tired."

"Okay. Well, I'll talk to y'all later."

My brother lived with my parents still, so my sister took the only other available bedroom. My other sister lived out of town and was only visiting a couple of months ago when all the kids were over. So, that left me with nowhere to go. Walking to my bedroom, Broderick got in front of me and went to his knees. "I'm begging you. Please don't leave. Don't take my girls away from me. I need to be able to see them every day."

But obviously not me. More salt to the wound. This wasn't about me. He wasn't begging for his wife of fifteen years to stay. He was begging for me not to take his daughters. Before I could walk around him, he wrapped his arms around my legs, squeezing them. Not thinking of the consequences, I popped the shit out of him in his head. He fell back to his heels in shock, but before he could address it, I collapsed to the floor. My legs were hurting so badly, they completely gave out on me. He nursed his wounds while I laid on the floor in pain. The girls must have heard the commotion because they came out of their room. "Mommy!"

They both ran to me, falling to their knees. "Are you okay? What's wrong?"

"My legs... my legs are hurting so bad."

"Should I call 9-1-1?"

"No. She's okay. I'm gonna get her to the bed," Broderick said.

I really didn't want him touching me. I would lay on the floor all night, but my girls were watching. He didn't want to help me up either. I could see it in his eyes. It was his fault. He knew better than squeezing my legs that way. It literally felt like there was no blood circulating through them. However, every doctor I'd been to, had told me that my circulation was great and that it was the neuropathy and my fluctuating glucose levels that kept me in so much pain. The excess fluid didn't help either.

He put his arms around my upper torso, underneath my arms and yanked me up. I groaned in pain as I tried to stand on my legs. But they were so wobbly and weak, there was no way they could support me. He picked me up by wrapping his arms around my waist and practically threw me to the bed. I grimaced in pain, not wanting to curse him out in front of my girls. "Daddy! You hurt Mommy! Why did you throw her?" Tiana yelled.

Zahria hit him on his arm and I could tell she'd done it as hard as she could. Their dad picked with me all the time, but most times they thought he was playing. "Your mama is heavy. I handled her the best way I could."

I turned my back to him and laid there with my eyes closed. My girls took my shoes off and Tiana said, "Don't worry, Mommy. We're gonna take care of you. Do you need anything?"

"Just my medicine and some water, baby. Thank you."

"You're welcome. Which medicine?"

"I have a bottle in my purse."

She rummaged through it and found the bottle as Zahria helped me undress. I hated that my children felt like they had to take care of me. If that wasn't depressing, I didn't know what was. Broderick had left the room. If I wanted to leave anyway, I couldn't right now.

My legs weren't cooperating, so I had no choice but to stay here tonight. Broderick came back in the room and got a blanket and a pillow, then said to me, "I'll leave tomorrow."

He walked out of the room as Zahria asked, "Where's Daddy going tomorrow?"

"I don't know, but we aren't getting along, girls. Your dad and I are breaking up."

The sadness on their faces brought me to tears and they succumbed to tears of their own. "Will we live with you? And will we get to see Daddy?"

"Yes and yes. Things will be better that way. I know you guys hear us arguing all the time and I hate that."

"Okay, Mommy," Tiana said. "Can we sleep with you tonight?"

"If you promise to do your best to not kick me in your sleep," I said with a smirk.

Their faces lit up because they hadn't been able to sleep with me in a long time. Their kicks in their sleep often landed on my feet and legs. After taking my pill, they got in bed with me and turned on the TV as I messaged East. *I hope the rest of your dinner went well. He's leaving tomorrow.*

CHAPTER 10

E aston

WHEN I GOT NELLY'S MESSAGE, I'D JUST DROPPED WHITNEY home. She was angry as hell. According to her, I should have checked my mama. Then she informed me that I couldn't hide my love for the slow-walking chick. After I checked her, because I knew she was being funny, she really copped a whole attitude. She said, *See how you jumped to her defense? Why didn't you do that for me? This proves that your mom was right.*

After she had her rant, I was ready to get rid of her ass. When I got to the car and saw Nelly's message, I could feel her hurt through every word of it. I knew she was married and that her heart was still his, but shit... my heart didn't seem to care. I wanted to be there for her, no matter how long she went without talking to me. Before pulling off, I responded, *The dinner was fine. How are you feeling, Nelly?*

I was prepared to see her be evasive and lie to me, but I was surprised when she messaged back, *I'm not feeling good at all, East. Physically, I'm in pain. My legs are so weak, I can't stand right now. Mentally, I'm drained. Emotionally, I'm hurting and spiritually, I'm broken. How did I get here? It's like my entire life blew by and I didn't get to really enjoy it like I should have. I've always catered to everyone else, but now that I need catering to, no one is available. I've always been the strong one, but where does the strong go when they get weak?*

Rubbing my hand down my face, I exhaled loudly. It was hard not being there for her. After giving her words some thought, I typed out my response. *It's time for you to come to me, Nelly. Let me be everything you desire in a man. Let me take care of you and the girls. I love you and I wanna be there for you. Tell me where you are, and I'll come get y'all.*

After I hit the send button, I drove away, sitting on pins and needles, waiting for what she would say. I knew she wasn't ready to dive in like I was, but I was hoping that she would allow me to be a friend to her at least. Despite my feelings for her, I just wanted her to be good... get her health on track and her mental refocused. Whatever happened after that would be up to her. By the time I got home, I heard my phone chime. Quickly grabbing it, I opened the message. *I love you, too, East. You know that, but I can't let you get involved in all this shit.*

I was already involved. Just knowing what all she was going through had me on edge. If I knew where she lived, I'd confront that dude. That was just how pissed I was about it and I didn't even know the details. I continued reading, *If it's okay, the girls and I will come by tomorrow.*

Maybe I could convince her face to face of where she should be. As long as she stayed in that house, he was going to give her a hard time. *Of course, it's okay. I'll cook spaghetti. Do the girls like spaghetti?*

Yeah, but Tiana only likes noodles and sauce, no meat. Can you put her some noodles and sauce to the side before you mix it?

I smiled slightly. I couldn't wait to get to know them and cater to them. While I knew I was jumping the gun, my heart was excited. That was only gonna set me up for failure, but I had to try. I responded to her message. *Of course, I can. I can't wait to spend time with y'all tomorrow.*

I wondered if the girls knew what was going on. Tiana seemed to be really mature for her age and Zahria was the baby of the two. She was actually more like an eight-year-old. Tiana was only nine, but she had the maturity of a teenager. She seemed to tend to Nel's physical needs while Zahria tended to her emotional needs. They shouldn't have to do that when their dad and her husband was in the same house. He ignored the duties required of him as a husband and left it to his daughters who shouldn't have to worry about anything other than being kids.

Tomorrow, I would cater to all three of them, showing Nelly how much I love her and how I would take care of her and the girls if she let me. She didn't have to say she wanted to be in a relationship. Just so long as she kept coming around, allowing me to be there for the three of them. My soul would be happy to know that God saw fit to bless me with three perfect women. As I turned in my driveway, my phone started ringing. Thinking it was Nelly, I hurriedly answered the phone. "Hello?"

"You ain't fooling me. What's going on with you and Nel?"

Had I not been driving, I would have closed my eyes. "What are you talking 'bout, Ma?"

"You know exactly what I'm talking about, Easton. That girl is married. I don't care how unhappy she may be, you are going to get hurt. I know she's your friend, but you can't cross into forbidden territory. I was in this very situation with the man that donated the sperm for you. He was married, convincing me of how unhappy he was and that he would leave his wife. That never happened, baby. But you know all that. Don't follow in my footsteps."

"It's a lil different with me and Nelly, though. We've been friends forever."

"Aww shit. You already crossed the line, haven't you?"

I exhaled loudly. "Yeah. I'm in love with her. But I knew the risk when I got involved, Ma. I'ma grown man and I'll handle it accordingly."

"You're gonna get hurt."

"Most likely, but maybe next lifetime, she'll be for me."

I could imagine her rolling her eyes. "There you go with that poetic mess. Boy, next lifetime, I pray you in heaven, giving glory to God for saving yo' soul. Quit chasing after Nelly. She ain't ready for the love you have to give. I would have loved to have her as a daughter-in-law, but the time has passed on that. I know you have tough skin and you try to act all hard, but I'm yo' mama. Remember that. I know yo' ass."

"A'ight, Ma. I appreciate you. Thank you again for a great dinner."

I was tired of the conversation and I knew the only way to get her to stop talking about it was to get off the phone. I knew the risk, but I didn't care. Maybe we would be the one percent of people that it worked for. There was only one way to find out.

"SORRY, WE GOT A LATE START, BUT WE'LL BE THERE WITHIN AN hour."

"It's okay. I just finished cooking. How are you feeling?"

"I'm better than I was yesterday evening. Let me finish Z's hair and we'll be heading your way."

"A'ight. Bring overnight bags for you and the girls."

"East, I'on—"

"Nelly. You trust me?"

"Yes."

"Bring overnight bags for you and the girls. I promise, I got y'all."

"Okay."

I ended the call and texted her my address. I didn't know if she remembered how to get here. Her husband had definitely left already since she actually called me. I had the entire day planned for us. I'd gotten an electric blanket and some CBD oil to rub on her feet and legs. I'd also bought a fresh deck of Uno cards, ice cream, and cookies. Netflix was cued up, waiting for them to pick us a movie.

Although I had to work tomorrow, I didn't have to be there until ten. I'd cook them a great breakfast in the morning and just cater to their needs, taking their minds off their troubles. I busied myself making iced tea and Kool-Aid, then made a salad and slid cheesy garlic bread in the oven. Checking everything for a second time, making sure everything was laid out for them... perfect for what they could want, I smiled. Taking the mugs from the freezer I'd bought for the girls, I poured Kool-Aid in them. One had Elsa on the outside and the other had Anna. Hopefully, they liked the movie Frozen.

By the time I started plating their food, the doorbell rang, and I was excited as hell. This was so damn new for me. I'd never been this tender with anybody, and kids weren't even a thought. My heart was invested in something I would probably never see the rewards of. When I opened the door, those thoughts all went out the window as I smiled at the three beautiful women standing on my doorstep. "Hey! Y'all come in!" I said excitedly, trying to make the girls comfortable.

They all smiled and stepped inside. Once I closed the door, I glanced at the duffle bags on their shoulders and said, "Let me take those. Are y'all ready to have fun?"

The girls smiled brightly, and a slight smile made its way to Nelly's face as well. Zahria said, "Yes, sir!"

"Get comfortable while I put your bags away."

They all sat on the couch as I made my way down the hallway, my heart beating out of my fucking chest. I didn't know why I was so nervous. After dropping them on the bed, I made my way back to them. Nelly was talking softly to them as they stared into her face intently. When she saw me, she stopped talking. "Are y'all ready to eat?"

"Yes, sir," the girls said in unison.

"Okay. Come to the table and I'll bring your food out."

"Let me help you, East."

"No. I want you to relax. Stay off your feet as much as possible until I can take care of you later."

Her face reddened a bit and she smiled slightly, then sat at the table. After asking their preferences for salad, I brought their drinks to them. The girls' eyes widened as they noticed the cartoon characters on their jars. They giggled, then switched cups. They were familiar with Frozen. I sat a small glass of tea and a bottle of water for Nelly on the table as well. When I sat their food in front of them, the girls were about to dig in until Nelly halted them. "Wait for East to join us."

I smiled as I headed their way with my plate and glass of tea. Once I sat, Nelly asked, "East, do you mind if I bless the food?"

"Not at all. Go ahead."

We all bowed our heads and she began, "Thank you, Lord, for blessing us to be in great company. Bless the owner of this home, who has so graciously opened it up to me and my daughters. Thank you for his hospitality and his heart. We ask that you would bless this food and especially bless the person who cooked it. We're extremely grateful to have someone in our corner. In Your name, Amen."

When I lifted my head, our eyes met. She cleared her throat and said, "East, this looks amazing."

"Thank you. Y'all eat up, because we got things to do! Uno, ice cream, cookies, movies... we 'bout to turn up."

The girls laughed as Nelly shook her head and took her first forkful of spaghetti. Her eyes closed for a moment, then she said, "This is really good, East."

"Thank you, beautiful."

The girls' eyes immediately landed on mine. *Shit.* They looked at each other, then Tiana said, "Thank you for not putting meat in mine."

I smiled at her and said, "You're welcome, gorgeous."

She blushed and continued eating. Not wanting to be left out, Zahria said, "The garlic bread is really good."

I smiled at her and said, "Thank you, gorgeous."

She blushed as well while Nelly smiled. Hopefully, that fixed it. They wouldn't think I had a thing for their mom. That was a stupid thought. Kids were a lot smarter than adults gave them credit for. They knew I had a thing for their mama and there was nothing I could say to convince them otherwise, nor did I want to.

CHAPTER 11

N elsondra

THEIR LAUGHTER MADE ME SMILE AND I WAS BEYOND HAPPY THAT we'd come to East's house. I was soaking in the tub, listening to them play Connect Four. We'd eaten food, dessert, watched a movie and had played Uno. After that, he told the girls he was going to run me a bath so I could soak, then he would be back to play more games with him. That was what he was doing. I was beyond grateful for East taking their minds off their jackass for a father. He made a whole fucking production this morning.

He had two duffle bags and was crying, hugging the girls like he wasn't gonna ever see them again. I could have kicked him in his mouth. That irritated the fuck out of me. They were crying, not realizing the bastard was just going to his parents' house two minutes down the street. I was so ready to get them away from everything. So, when East asked us to bring an overnight bag, I was happy.

But my phone had been going off almost the entire time we'd been here. I refused to answer his calls, so he'd been texting, asking about the girls like he didn't just see them this morning and wanting to talk to them. After the bullshit he pulled this morning, he'd better pray they talked to him tomorrow. After washing myself, I was trying to get out of the tub on my own, when someone knocked on the door. "Can I come in?" East asked.

"Yeah."

He walked in with a smile, but when he saw me on my knees in the tub, he rushed over to me. "Let me help you, Nelly. The girls are having a great time. They make me wish I would have had children."

"Why didn't you?"

"I'on know. Never found a woman who I wanted to be that close to or start a family with."

When I was in a standing position, I dried off and put on my wide-legged pajama pants and a top, only nodding in response to what he'd said. Before I could leave the bathroom, he pulled me close and kissed my lips. "I really missed you, Nel. I can tell you wanna talk, so we can do that once the girls go to sleep."

"You have to work tomorrow. We can talk whenever."

He kissed my forehead and said, "Okay. I'm gonna go get the oil."

I went back to the front with the girls to see them concentrating hard as they played Connect Four. They were having a great time and I was glad they were enjoying themselves. East appeared behind me and he lightly rubbed the back of my neck, setting my soul on fire. "Let's get you to feeling better, baby," he said softly, sounding like Michael Ealy in my ear.

Had my girls not been with me, I would have taken all these clothes off. Going to the couch, they noticed us and headed my way. "Mommy, how was your bath?"

"It was amazing. Maybe Mr. East will let the two of you take a bath in his big tub."

"Ooooh, is like yours, Mommy?"

"Yep."

They were jumping in excitement and I winked at East as he narrowed his eyes at me. I wanted alone time with him, and I couldn't wait for the girls to go to sleep to get it. Just my luck, they would be up all night and I would be asleep before them. East was my only real friend and confidant. This anguish and disappointment I felt was weighing me down, although I was doing my best to hide it in front of my daughters. "Mr. East, can we?" Tiana asked.

"Of course. Let me start the water running."

When he stood to go to the bathroom, I felt my phone vibrating next to me. Looking at it, I expected to see Broderick's name and number. But instead of rolling my eyes, I decided to answer it, since it was my mama. "Hello?"

"Nel? Everything okay?"

"Hey, Ma. I'm okay. Why do you ask?"

"Broderick just called looking for you. He said you and the girls were gone and you weren't answering his calls."

"We've been fighting, Ma. He left this morning. We left the house shortly after he did to get away for a while."

"Nel... I'm so sorry. Is it something you guys can work on? Where are y'all?"

"I don't think it's gonna work this time, Ma. The girls and I are at Easton's house."

"Easton? The Easton that graduated with you?"

"Yes, ma'am."

"I didn't know he was in Beaumont," she said excitedly. "But umm... do you think it's wise that you be around another man while you're feeling so vulnerable, Nel?"

"I don't know if it is or isn't, but I *do* know that I'm tired of putting everyone else before me. When do I get to do what I want without worrying about what anyone else will think of it? I'm tired of being disrespected, verbally assaulted, and physically neglected. Always being told that I'm overreacting. My own husband isn't attracted to me anymore and to hear that come from his mouth... it was one of the most hurtful things he's ever said to me."

I looked over at the girls to see they were finishing up their game of Connect Four and I noticed East standing in the hallway, watching me as I bore my soul to my mother. The tears fell down my cheeks as she said, "I'm sorry, Nel. I didn't mean to upset you. Why didn't you come here?"

"I know that Tanya and Jonathan are there. The house would be entirely too crowded if we would have come over, too."

"Nel, we are always here for you. Just because we like Broderick, you're our daughter. We will always have your back, baby."

"I have to go. I'll talk to you later, Mama."

"Okay. I love you."

"I love you, too."

I could tell East wanted to console me, but he could do that in just a minute. "Who's ready to take a bath?"

The girls screamed in excitement as I said, "Get your under-clothes and pajamas before you go in there. We aren't at home."

At home, they'd strip naked in their bedrooms and walk through the house naked. They were at the age where I didn't even want them doing that in front of Broderick anymore. Tiana had almost as much pubic hair as I did and they'd both been wearing bras for the past two years. Deciding to go help them, I stood and walked to the hallway, standing directly in front of East. Resting my forehead on his shoulder for a minute, I walked past him. Just as I figured, Zahria was getting undressed. "Girls, remember we talked about who the only people were that were allowed to see y'all naked?"

"Yes, ma'am."

"Okay. Who are they?"

"You, Daddy, Granny, and Nana."

"And not even Daddy anymore. Y'all are growing up. You are becoming young ladies. But Mr. East isn't on that list, right?"

"Right."

"So, you can't get undressed in here and walk to the bathroom naked."

"I told you, Zahria." Tiana turned to me and said, "I told her that and she told me that I wasn't the boss of her."

I rolled my eyes. Zahria was always trying to be independent because Tiana was always trying to tell her what to do. "It's okay, Zahria. Just remember what Mommy said, okay?"

"Okay, Mommy."

I helped them bring their things into the bathroom to see East had run them a bubble bath as well. Going to the tub, I tested the water on my wrist. "Mommy, is Mr. East gonna be your new husband?" Tiana asked.

My eyebrows went up in surprise and I said, "Mr. East and I are friends."

"I think he likes you. He helps you a lot. More than Daddy."

I frowned slightly. "What do you mean, more than your daddy?"

I was testing the waters to see what she knew. It seemed I wasn't hiding my disdain for their father as well as I thought I was if she noticed the faults. "Daddy never really helps you. Just me and Zahria. Mr. East wouldn't even let you help bring plates to the table."

"I'm sorry, girls. I'm only friends with Mr. East. Will it ever be more than that? I don't know. Right now, I'm just trying to feel better about myself. Your dad and I are separating. That doesn't mean that either of us love the two of you any less. He loves y'all. Okay?"

"Okay," they said sadly.

After kissing both their heads, I left them inside, closing the door. I leaned against it and allowed the tears to escape me. Before I could gather my composure, East was standing in front of me. When I lifted my head, he grabbed my hands and led me to the front room where he had the oils on the table and a throw on the sofa. Upon further inspection, I noticed it was an electric blanket. I hadn't seen one of those in ages. "Lay down, baby. I can see you're hurt. Just relax and let me take care of you."

"Can you kiss me first?"

"Hell yeah."

He leaned in and gently laid his lips on mine as I wrapped my arms around his neck. When I heard the bathroom door, I pulled away from him as Zahria said, "Mommy."

"I'm coming, baby."

That was a sign. What was I doing besides playing with East's emotions? When I got to the door, she asked, "Where are the towels? Mr. East only put out one small towel."

I smiled at her and went to the cabinet and handed her one. "Enjoy your bath," I said, then winked at her.

When I made it back to the front, East was standing there,

waiting for me to return. I smiled at him and rubbed his cheek. "Lay down, Nel."

I did as he asked and he went to his knees, pushing my pants leg up. Why did East have to come back into my life now, when everything was in turmoil? Emotionally, I wasn't ready to be what he needed. Shit, I was still married. East wasn't spending as much time on my legs this time, but I knew he was trying to hurry before the girls got out of the tub. He was so perfect, but I couldn't enjoy the luxury of relaxing in the moment.

When he finished, he went to his bedroom with the oils and to wash his hands. Once he came back, he helped me sit up and draped the blanket over my legs and turned it on. Before he could sit next to me, the doorbell rang. He frowned, then looked at the time. It was almost eight o'clock. "Be right back."

When he opened the door, there was quietness, then I heard, "Tell Nel to come out here right fucking now!"

"You gon' calm down that tone. Your daughters are in there."

"You not gon' fucking tell me what to do or how to behave with my daughters."

I quickly made my way to my feet, faster than I had since I'd had neuropathy and almost ran to the door. "Broderick, what are you doing here?"

He glanced at me from head to toe. "I knew you were fucking him and now you got my daughters around this nigga? Send my children out here now!"

"Leave me the hell alone! You're the one that fucked up. How did you find me?"

He held his phone up, reminding me of the damn app for the car. How could I have been so stupid? "If you not gon' send my daughters out, I'm coming in to get them."

"I'd hate to get in the middle, because I don't know you, but you ain't coming in my house," East said.

Fuck! Fuck! Fuck! This was all my fault. "Broderick, just leave. They will see you tomorrow."

"My daughters are not staying here. They don't know this man and neither do I."

"Fuck you. You think I would put my babies in harm's way? This is how I know we're done this time. You clearly moved on a long time ago, but you always wanna make me miserable. I've been miserable for a long time. Now that I'm trying to be at peace with my best friend, you wanna be an ass. I know you remember me talking about East years ago when we first met."

Broderick tried to barge through the doorway, trying to get at me and East blocked him from entering. He swung at East as I did my best not to scream. Broderick barely missed him, and East pushed him backwards. "Stop! Please stop!"

"I'm sorry, East. We have to go. I never wanted to bring this shit to your house or even get you involved."

"You don't have to leave, Nelly," he said, slightly turning to me.

When he did, Broderick punched him. They started fighting right there in the doorway again and I screamed, "I'm gonna call the police! Broderick stop!"

East had put him in a headlock and he just held him for a moment, then threw him to the ground as he stretched his jaw. This was it. I would forever be alone in this world. East slammed the door shut and went to the kitchen to get ice and I went to the room to get our things. "Mommy, are we leaving?"

"Yeah."

"Aww. Why are you crying?"

I shook my head. I couldn't tell my daughters that their mother was stupid.

CHAPTER 12

E aston

I HAD A HEADACHE OUT OF THIS WORLD. MY JAW WASN'T noticeably swollen, but I couldn't sleep last night. All I could think about was the way Nelly and the girls left out of here last night. No matter how many times I asked her to stay, she refused. The girls were crying and so was she. She just kept saying how sorry she was. Before they could walk out of the door, I didn't care if the girls saw at that point, I pulled her close, hugging her tightly. They hadn't seen that between their parents in a while and I wanted them to remember what it looked like. I kissed her head, then released her.

That sorry excuse for a husband had already left when they walked out the door. I again begged her to stay. She declined. It was only because of her and her children that I didn't fuck him all the way up. We were having such an amazing time before he arrived. I'd planned to hold her for most of the night and listen to her talk about a man that didn't deserve her. Seeing the tears on their faces was a lot to take in. I'd been calling her since last night, but she wasn't

89

answering my calls or text messages. I was worried about her. I didn't know if he'd ever hit her or not and seeing how violent he was towards me didn't make matters any better.

Work had been busy at least. While it didn't help me to stop thinking about Nelly, it had helped the time pass by quickly. I'd made up in my mind that I would go to her parents' house when I got off work. I wasn't trying to get further involved in their shit, but I needed to know that she was okay. As I wrapped up the car deal I was working on, I huffed. My head hadn't let up and I knew I was gonna have to take Tylenol for it. I hated taking medicine of any kind. So, I chose to deal with pain as best I could until I had no choice but to take something to relieve it.

Shaking the customer's hand, I apologized for being quiet and informed them of my headache. I didn't want them to think that I was being rude. Pulling the drawer on my desk open, I realized I didn't have anything to take. Making a quick walk to accounting, I knew one of the ladies back there would have something I could take. Sure enough, several offered remedy. I took three Tylenol and headed back to my desk only to see Whitney in the waiting area. I was next on the list for a customer. She smirked at me as I called her in.

After sitting in my chair, she sat across from me and said, "You look like shit."

Looking at her bad weave, I said, "So do you."

The salesman's eyes widened as he said, "I take it y'all know each other."

I stared up at him until he caught the hint and walked away. Whitney sat in front of me as I looked over her paperwork, then thought better of it. "I'ma have to pass your deal to someone else."

"Why?"

"I don't wanna know this much about you. Because of our past relationship, this is against policy anyway."

She rolled her eyes, then stood from her seat as I gave her car deal back to her salesman who was waiting outside the door. "I can't see her financials. Against policy."

He frowned slightly as my eyes widened slightly. It wasn't against policy, but I didn't need her filing a complaint against me, either. I was communicating with him silently, to go along with me. "Yeah, you're right. I'll bring her to Dwayne."

"Thanks, man," I said as I gave Whitney a look.

The look that said, *you ain't shit*. Had she been respectful when she stepped in my office, her car deal would have been nearly done. She had a preapproval, which meant I wouldn't have had to wait for approval from a lender. I sat at my desk as I waited for the next customer to make their way to finance. As I did, my mama texted me. *What happened last night? You never called me.*

I rolled my eyes. She was the last person I wanted to explain this situation to, but since I didn't want to tell Aaron all Nelly's personal business, I would make a trip to her house after I left the Allison's residence. After responding to my mama, letting her know I would be by after work, I texted Nelly. *I just want to know you're okay, Nel. Please just give me that.*

After I sat my phone down, my next customer came in and I just prayed that all was well.

"I TOLD YOU NOT TO GET INVOLVED LIKE THAT WITH NELSONDRA. Why are you so damn hardheaded? That was a moment of trauma those precious angels could have done without. You and Nel need to stop thinking about yourselves right now and think about those babies. Can you imagine how hard this is for them?"

I exhaled and dragged my hand down my face, something I'd found myself doing quite often these days. It was never my intent to cause them more distress. If anything, all I'd wanted to do was get their minds off the drama at home and show them a good time. That was it. "I *was* thinking about them. I just wanted them to have a great time without having to think about what was going on at home and to take care of Nel. She's sick, Ma. Diabetes is raging through her body like it's out for revenge and neuropathy is creeping its way up her legs. I just wanted to be a distraction for them. That's it. I wasn't thinking about me."

She sat next to me and grabbed my hand. "Baby, how long as she had diabetes and neuropathy?"

"She's been diabetic for twenty years. But neuropathy didn't set in until two years ago in her feet. Her health has only declined since then. She's prone to infections. Her doctor recently put her on a fluid pill and blood pressure medicine. Nel is so stressed out in her marriage and that's only contributing to her health decline. Her health has gotten so bad until she works from home. She said she rarely feels like going anywhere."

Thinking about the bandage on her leg when I oiled her legs gave me pause. She'd said that she didn't have to pack her wound anymore and I was glad she was healing well. I hated all the changes she was going through, especially without the support of her husband. It was killing me not knowing how she was doing. Her parents weren't home when I went by there before coming to my mama's house. I was hoping they would have been because I still didn't know if she was okay. "That's so sad, but as long as she's married, you're gonna have to back off, son."

"Yeah."

"You've had sex with her. Haven't you?"

I glanced at my mama, wishing I wasn't having this conversation with her. "Once."

"Dammit, boy. She's married. It doesn't matter how unhappily. I love Nel and those girls, but I love you more."

"Mama, I told you before, I can handle it. But last night, seeing how happy the girls were when we played Uno, watched a movie, ate ice cream... that's enough to make a nigga fuck her husband up." I glanced at her widened eyes. "I'm sorry for my language."

"You're in love with a woman you can't have, son. If you need a distraction, there are plenty women—"

"Naw. I don't need a distraction. You invited one to my party. She looked like she used to be a man."

She slapped my arm playfully as she chuckled. She knew that shit was true. I chuckled along with her as my phone chimed. Quickly pulling it from my pocket, I saw a message from Nelly. *I'm okay. This fuck nigga had blocked you through Verizon's website. I swear, I'm starting to*

hate his ass. I've been searching for apartments for me and the girls and we
plan to sell this house so we can divide the assets.

I exhaled a sigh of relief. "Thank God."

"What?"

"I hadn't heard from her and I was nervous. She's okay. They're okay."

"Let me see your cheek."

I turned my head so she could get a good look at it. "It ain't that bad. He hit like a punk."

She chuckled and shook her head. "So... what'chu gon' do? Because I know my son and I know you ain't gon' leave her be."

"Leave her be? You sound like you resurrecting slave dialect."

"Shut up, Easton. You know what I'm staying. Quit stalling."

"Mama, I can't quit checking on her unless she tells me to stop. Until then, I'm gon' continue to be there when she needs me. I don't care about her nigga. If he was doing what he was supposed to, we would have never went there. But I'm glad we went there."

My mind went back to that night... how she let me make love to her and how wet her pussy was. Although she was slightly inebriated, I knew that it was something she'd really wanted. She had yet to discuss a moment of regret about that night. Actually, we didn't talk about it. I don't recall having a conversation about what happened between us at all. We just kind of went on about our lives. I felt like maybe she regretted it since she didn't talk to me for a minute afterwards, but she didn't *say* that she regretted it. "Boy, snap out of it!"

I looked over at my mama and she rolled her eyes and shook her head. "Jesus Christ himself gon' have to come down and slap some sense into your ass."

I chuckled softly, then messaged Nel back. *Are the girls okay?*
Yes. Can I call you?

She answered quick as hell and that made me nervous. "I gotta go, Ma. It's been a long day and I'm tired as hell. I'll call you tomorrow."

"Uh-huh," she said, sounding like Jennifer Lewis.

She often reminded me of her, and it didn't help that they resembled, wide smile and all. I kissed her cheek, then stood as I messaged Nelly. *Of course.*

Before I could get in my car good, she was calling. Maybe her husband was gone like she said. If so, I was glad she finally chose herself over his bullshit. "Hello?"

She broke down crying, causing me to halt my forward progress. "Whoa, what's wrong?"

"I need to get away from here. Me and my girls are going out of town. I need some peace. When I heard your voice, I realized how much peace it brought me. But I can't depend on you for peace. I need to find that within myself. This house wreaks of memories from the past two years and it feels like I'm gonna suffocate."

"Let me come pick y'all up."

"I can't do that. He knows where you live. I never wanted to bring bullshit like that to your doorstep, East. I love you too much for that. I'm so sorry about last night."

"What if I got y'all a hotel room?"

"I'm gonna go to Houston. Maybe get a room for a couple of nights. I feel like I'm dying."

"Let me come get you, Nel. Please? Is he there?"

"No. He's not here. I'm okay, East. Just stay on the phone with me."

"Where are the girls?"

"They're in their room, on their tablets. They wear headphones, so I doubt that they can hear me."

"Maybe now that the three of you are alone, you should consider telling them to take their headphones off in case you need them. If something happens, like you falling, you can scream for them. How are your legs and feet?"

"They're okay, I guess. I've been in bed all day. I just haven't felt like moving."

"Listen. I know you're going through a rough time, but I don't want you to fall into a depression that you can't get yourself out of. I love you, Nel, and I hate to hear you this way. I'm in love wit'chu, baby. So, please at least try to move around. For me, please."

I could hear her cry harder. Closing my eyes, I listened to her cries and did my best to stomach them. How was I supposed to convince her to let me be there for her? I didn't give a fuck about Broderick. "Can I book a hotel in Houston for the weekend and maybe you and the girls can meet me there? I can book it for Saturday."

"Book it for Friday. I don't want him to see us leave. Let me give you my credit card information."

"Nel. I got'chu."

She never responded to my confession and I knew that it was because she was still in love with her husband of fifteen years. However, if I had my way, I would show her how a woman was supposed to be treated... cherished and adored. It went so much deeper than sex and I needed her to understand how entangled our souls were. This was meant to happen. Her marriage went to hell to make room for me. While I talked to myself on the regular, trying to check my sanity levels when it came to Nel, I knew that I was right. Whether Nel would be open to accept it or not was another story.

CHAPTER 13

N elsondra

"THAT NIGGA TELLING THE WHOLE LOCKER ROOM ABOUT HAVING SEX with me? That's why I shouldn't have entertained his ass. All that shit he was talking on his dick and I could barely feel the shit."

East chuckled, then said, "I know I shouldn't be laughing, but I could have told you that shit if you would have asked. That shit look like a grub-worm with a turtleneck on."

"What in the fuck is a grubworm, East?"

"Look it up in the library at school tomorrow. I bet that shit make you feel better. You gon' laugh hard as hell. Loudmouth muthafucka. I handled him, though. You ain't got to worry about hearing nobody repeat that shit, I promise."

I laid back in East's arms, sitting on the swing on the porch at home. He was always here for me. Why couldn't he feel how much I loved him? Maybe trying to be with him would ruin our friendship and I surely couldn't handle that. East was my best friend and there was no way I would find anybody that meant more to me than he did. I had other friends, but none of them were as close to me as he was. "Now, come on, let's play a game or something before one of your peeps come home and think we doing shit. You know yo' mama always got her good eye on me. Talking 'bout I gotta get up early in the morning to get one over on her."

I laughed at him imitating my mama's voice. "You crazy. Let's play a game of badminton. It'll make me feel better to beat your ass."

"I'm an athlete, Nel, but birdies ain't big enough to hit. You only wanna play because you know I have a hard time seeing that shit."

I laughed. "Hell yeah. It's the one sport I know I can beat you at. You supposed to be making me feel better, right?"

He rolled his eyes as he followed me to the backyard. I spun around and fell into him, wrapping my arms around his neck. "Thank you, East, for always having my back."

He kissed my forehead and said, "Always, sweetheart."

When I pulled away from him, I saw something in his eyes, but I knew I had to have imagined it. East didn't want me. He wanted those big-ass, big-titty hoes. Looking away, I said, "A'ight. Let's start this therapy session in match one on yo' ass."

When I woke up, I nearly hopped out of my damn skin. Broderick was sitting in the bed, staring at me. That shit made me nervous as hell. Knowing what I was just dreaming about, I was praying that I wasn't talking in my sleep. "What are you doing here?"

"I came to offer one last-ditch effort at salvaging our marriage. You know I love you. I fucked up. I can admit that. I fucked up big time and I have been for a while now. You don't deserve the shit I been dishing out. I took you for granted and I'm done with pretending that you hadn't been my world for the past nineteen years. Since the day I met you, I knew you would be the woman to change my life. And you did, Nel. Can you please give us one more chance?"

"No. Nothing is gonna change and I'm tired of giving chance after chance only for you to hurt me over and over again. The shit is exhausting and it's taking a toll on me physically, spiritually and emotionally. I'm drained and I don't even have the energy to put into our marriage. I don't trust you anymore. Your words and apologies mean nothing to me. They are all words I've heard repeatedly for the past year and a half and I'm fucking tired. Please don't come in here without knocking again."

"This my fucking house, too. I can come and go as I please. I sleep down the street at my parents' house to appease you. But I can very well stay here. Fuck outta here with that shit."

"And there's the real Broderick. I was wondering when he was gonna show up. Don't worry. I've been looking for places to stay and the girls and I will be out of here before you know it. I also have an attorney. I suggest you get one as well."

"This is fucking stupid. All because you want somebody to wait on you hand and foot."

"No! It's because I want a muthafucka to respect me and actually give a damn about my heart! Somebody I shouldn't even have to ask for those things from. You were supposed to love me! What in the fuck happened to that?"

"Your illness is too much for me! There, I said it! It's too much for me to handle. I feel like I'm missing something, and I don't like that feeling."

"Then why are you trying to work it out?"

"For the sake of our children."

When he said that, I glanced toward the hallway to see them standing in my doorway with tears streaming down their faces. I closed my eyes briefly, then said, "Come here, babies. I'm sorry."

As they walked over to me, I looked back at Broderick. "And you wanna stay together so they can see and hear us fight all the time? You see what this is doing to them?"

He exhaled loudly, then left the room. Holding my babies close, I kissed them repeatedly. They climbed in the bed with me and I said, "I'm sorry, girls."

"Mommy, why do y'all argue so much?" Tiana asked.

"We just can't seem to agree about how to solve issues that we're having, baby. Why don't y'all go brush your teeth and we may go visit Granny and Grampy today."

"Yay!" Zahria yelled.

I kissed their cheeks, then laid back in bed. Today was the day we were going to Houston for the weekend. As soon as Broderick left for work, we would be out of here. I didn't want to risk him following me. Although he could look to see where I was on that damned app... *Shit!* I grabbed my phone and looked at the app to figure out how to change the password. While I knew it was on my phone, too, I rarely used it. My app was giving me issues, but since the only thing I used it for was to remote start the car, I didn't make a big deal about it. I was never that far away from my car to where I couldn't use the key fob to remote start it.

After fooling with it for a few minutes, I'd successfully changed the password. A devious smile spread across my face. *Fuck wit' it, jackass.* That small accomplishment had put me in a better mood. It was still early, but I decided that once we left from here today, we wouldn't be coming back to pack a damn bag. Once the girls came out of the bathroom, I told them to pack a bag with two days' worth of clothing and their swimsuits. The excitement on their faces made me smile. It didn't take much to excite them and I loved that.

After going to the bathroom and handling my hygiene, I proceeded to pack a bag as well. Sending a message to East, I typed, *Good morning. Have a good day at work.* He would be meeting us there tonight, but he wouldn't be sleeping in the same room with us. My girls were my main priority and I needed them to feel comfortable. I knew East was trustworthy, but him being in the same room with them would confuse them.

Once I was completely packed, I went and checked the girls' bags to see what they'd packed, then started combing hair. My phone chimed and I knew it was from East. He'd responded, *Good morning. I hope you're having a great day. Can't wait to see y'all.*

I smiled and continued combing hair. When I was done, we loaded the car with our bags, and I went back inside to be sure we had everything. Looking at the time to see it was almost eleven, I decided to take them to lunch before we went to my parents' house. They were probably just waking up anyway. Check-in at the hotel wasn't until three. We would leave about two, so we wouldn't get caught in the lunch traffic in Houston. When I got back to the car and started backing out, I noticed Broderick's truck in the street, about to turn in our driveway.

Rolling my eyes, I put my window down to see what he wanted. "What?"

"Where are y'all going?"

"To lunch, why?"

"Can I take y'all to lunch instead?"

I rolled my eyes. This nigga had to be stupid. Why was he like this? It was like in his mind, we weren't just having a serious argument. He'd just said I was too much for him to handle. I mouthed the words, *Fuck you,* then drove off. I kept looking in my rearview mirror to see if he was going to follow us. Switching the mirror to the actual mirror instead of the camera so I could see the girls, I noticed they had their headphones on and were engrossed in their tablets. *Good.*

Flipping the mirror back to camera mode, I saw his truck still sitting in the street. I bet he was trying to pull up his app. Chuckling softly, I continued driving, turning the corner quickly in case he tried to follow us. My phone began ringing and when I saw his number, I ignored it and I was on the verge of blocking his ass. I was so sick of him and this morning only solidified my decision to file for a divorce. He made it seem like caring for me was like taking care of an invalid. There were lots of things that I did for myself. I still cooked and cleaned. There were just times that I was in too much pain to do so.

His ass was lazy, and he didn't want to have to do anything besides go to work. It was tiring as hell and I was done with trying to please him. For the first time in our marriage, I needed him to be there for me and he couldn't. That shit was blowing me. The phone rang again as I turned on College Street, heading to the highway to take my baby to Cheddar's. They loved their spinach dip and we hadn't been in a while. Glancing at it, I noticed it was Broderick calling again. "What now?"

"My app isn't working. Did you change the password?"

"What do you need the app for, Broderick?"

He was quiet for a moment, realizing that he was telling on himself. *Idiot.* "I wanna make sure you're going where you said you're going."

"Why in the fuck does it matter? We're divorcing."

"Because you have my daughters. That's why it matters."

"Fuck you! You're the one that caused all of this! Why can't you see that? Go meet your woman so she can occupy your time."

I ended the call only to hear my babies crying in the backseat. That hurt my heart and it caused me to cry, too. I hated that they were hearing us fight all the time... not to mention the vulgar language that I couldn't help but spew whenever Broderick and I argued. This bullshit with him couldn't be over quick enough. But in my heart, I knew that it most likely would never be over. He would continue giving me a hard time even after our marriage was done.

❧

AS THE GIRLS GOT THEIR SWIMSUITS ON, THERE WAS A KNOCK AT the door. I knew that it was East. I was so excited, and the girls seemed excited as well. When I'd told them that East was gonna meet us here, they screamed in excitement. Looking through the peephole, I got a glimpse of East's natural frown that he often wore on his face. It was his natural look, but one would assume he was angry if they didn't know him. I quickly opened the door with a huge smile on my face, happy to see him. "Hey!"

"What's up?" he asked with a huge smile on his face.

The girls ran to him and asked, "Are you going to swim with us?"

"Swim? Y'all know how to swim?"

"Yes!" Zahria exclaimed as I rolled my eyes and shook my head.

East glanced up at me and I said, "They can't swim. They play in the water. With a vest on, Zahria thinks she can swim. Tiana doesn't even like water in her face."

"Hey! I can go underwater!" Tiana yelled playfully as I rolled my eyes.

They both giggled as East smiled big at them. "What about you, Nelly? You getting in?"

"No. The water will be too cold. If there's a jacuzzi down there, I'll get in that."

"Okay. Well, let me put on my swimming trunks. Give me five minutes," he said as he headed out the door.

Once he did, I went to the bathroom and put on my swimsuit, then a wrap to hide my cellulite. I was quite sure, no one wanted to see all of that. "Mommy?"

"Yeah, baby?"

"Is Mr. East your boyfriend?"

"No, Zahria. We're just friends."

Tiana smiled like she knew something she wasn't saying, then gave me one of those *uh huh* looks. "Listen, girls. East isn't my boyfriend. Does that mean he never will be? No. But right now, I'm focused on the two of you and making sure that the three of us heal from the separation from your dad. It's nice having East around, but he isn't my boyfriend. Okay?"

"Okay."

I knew this wouldn't be the last conversation about East, just like it wasn't the first, but that seemed to satisfy them as East knocked at the door again. After opening it, I noticed he had goggles, floaties, and all kinds of unnecessary bullshit. I shook my head as the girls screamed in excitement. "Wow!"

"You're trying to spoil them? Don't start something you can't finish, East."

"I finish everything I start. And some things I just wanna work on forever."

I had to be blushing because my face was hot as hell. Walking out to the hallway with him, we made our way to the elevator to head down to the pool. Zahria and Tiana rushed to it to be the first to touch the button. They were always wanting to be the first to push the button. East grabbed my hand and squeezed it, causing me to look up at him. "How are you, Nelly?"

"I'm making it. We had a run-in this morning. I have to get an apartment, because he won't respect my privacy in a house that's partially his. When I woke up this morning, he was lying next to me, staring at me. Scared the fuck outta me."

"Why don't y'all move in with me?"

I looked up at him as the elevator doors opened. Swallowing my emotions, I followed the girls on. "I can't do that, East."

"Why not?"

"It's not that simple. My heart is in pieces. It needs to be whole again before I can make another commitment."

"Nelly, I'm not asking for a commitment. I'm just trying to help. I have three bedrooms. Seeing you heartbroken and in pain is hard. You're walking with a limp today, so I know you're stressed and hurting."

He paid attention to me more than I thought he did. I was doing my best to hide the limp and trying not to wince. I was used to being in pain and it was something I learned to deal with. "Let me think about it, okay?" I asked as the elevator doors opened.

He nodded and grabbed my hand, leading me to the jacuzzi. "Girls, be careful. Don't go too far."

"Okay!"

As I stepped down into the hot water, I exhaled. My God, it felt amazing. When I sat, I closed my eyes and I felt East staring at me. "You're so beautiful, Nelly. But the sadness I can see in you is crippling. If it makes you feel better, I can help you look for an apartment. I don't want you to feel uncomfortable. Before anything else, we're friends and I'm just tryna look out for my friend."

He kissed my cheek, then left my side to go entertain the girls in the pool while I wished things were as easy for me as they were for him.

CHAPTER 14

E aston

I'D GONE TO MY ROOM TO TAKE A SHOWER WHILE NELLY TOOK her shower, then came back when the girls got in the tub. I could see her mind was troubled and all over the place. After rubbing her legs, I sat next to her and said, "Talk to me, baby. What's on your mind?"

"I just hate what my marriage has become. It's like he likes picking with me just to see how far he can go. I'm so tired of the bullshit. He doesn't seem to understand how much that shit irritates me."

"Maybe he does and that's why he does it."

"Well, he can go to hell. That shit only pushes me further away. It only makes me wish I would have left a long-ass time ago, when we got into all the other fights."

"Pick with you like how?"

"Stupid shit... like for example, I'd been gone with the girls and he beat us home. He'd been there at least an hour before us. I went to the kitchen and fixed the kids something to eat, but I wasn't hungry. I sat on the couch to watch TV with him and this nigga asked, *You ain't gon' bother to ask if I wanted to eat?* What the fuck? He was home a fucking hour or more before us."

I slowly shook my head. This dude had to be stupid. He was definitely lazy as fuck and spoiled. "After pointing out that he'd *been* home, I asked him if he was retarded. You know he had the nerve to get pissed? Didn't say shit else to me for the rest of the night. Went to the room and slammed the door. But my stupid ass stayed through the bullshit, thinking that it was minor. Well, when he constantly does minor shit like that, it becomes major."

Her face was red as the flames of hell. I gently rubbed her hand, then lifted it to my lips to kiss. There were no words for me to offer her. She knew how I felt about his ass. I never hid my opinion about anybody she fucked with.

"*You talking to Toby? Tell me that shit ain't true. That nigga fucking with several other girls. He talk about the shit in eighth period.*"

"*Yeah. We just started talking the other day. We're just talking, East. Calm down.*"

"*Naw. You tripping. That nigga ain't no good for you. And before you say the shit, I ain't hating. His ass just gon' hurt you, Nelly, or bring you back some shit you can't get rid of.*"

"*Who said anything about having sex with him?*"

"*I'm saying it just in case you thinking about it. You know you my girl. I don't wanna be trying to console you because he done burnt yo' ass.*"

She pushed me hard, but then looked at me with a smirk on her face. "You make me sick."

"*Yeah. I love yo' ass, too.*"

Too bad I wasn't around to get the filter off her lenses when she married his ass. She wouldn't be going through the heartache she was feeling. When she broke down, I couldn't help but pull her face into my hands and lay my lips on hers. She moaned softly as I slid my tongue in her mouth. However, the ringing of her phone caused her to pull away. Once she looked at it, she grabbed it and angrily threw it against the wall. It caught me off-guard because I'd never seen Nel this angry. She stood from the couch and went to the bathroom to check on the girls.

I could hear them talking to her quietly. Standing, I went to where she threw her phone and picked it up from the floor. The screen was cracked, but it looked like it could still be used. When she came out, she pushed me to the wall and began pulling my pants off. "Nelly, hol' on. What'chu doing?"

"They will yell for me when they're done. I told them that they couldn't come out naked and to let me help them get situated."

She sat on the bed and pulled me between her legs by my waist-band. I exhaled loudly as she slid her hand in my sweats and boxer briefs and grabbed ahold of my dick. Backing away from her, I said, "Naw. Not like this. You pissed and your children are in the next room."

She fell back to the bed and brought her hands to her face. Crawling in the bed with her, I pulled her to me and said, "I love you too much, Nel. I love your girls. Them being in this room won't even let me get hard. Look at me."

She lifted her head and stared up at me. "You're strong, baby. When you feeling weak, though, you know I got'chu. Not for sex, but for your heart. I know you fucked up about this shit with him. But I admire your strength. You gon' get through this, baby."

I kissed her lips as my hands slid down her back. As I held her around her waist, she laid against my chest until the girls were done with their bath.

◈

"How did you find us? I'm sick of you trying to hold on to what you're pushing away. Leave me alone before I call the police!"

I hopped up from the bed, not thinking about the consequences, but stopped at the door when I heard her door close. I continued listening, then heard him kick the door. "You can't keep my kids away from me, Nel!"

"It's only been a day, jackass!" I heard her yell from the room.

There was more banging on the door, and I wanted to come out of my room, but I knew that would only make matters worse for her. Going to the phone, I called the room number. "Hello?"

One of the girls answered and she was in tears. I knew they were scared. I couldn't understand why he couldn't just leave Nelly alone. She was gonna come back to town eventually. He was acting like he didn't know her. They'd been married fifteen years. "Hey, baby girl. Y'all okay?"

"We're scared. Are you coming help us, East?"

"Yeah. I'll be there in a minute."

Knowing what this could mean, I couldn't stay in my room any longer. Not after hearing her cries. I didn't even know which one I was talking to, but it didn't matter. Baby girl asked me to come help them. Just as I opened the door, I heard, "Sir, we're going to have to ask you to leave or we will be forced to call the police. You are disturbing our other guests."

Closing my door, so he wouldn't see me, I watched him walk to the elevator, wiping his face. That nigga had the nerve to cry. *What the fuck?* Something had to be wrong with his ass. Going back to the phone, I called their room number again. "Hello?"

"Nel, y'all okay?"

"I'm holding them now. I think I'm gonna file a restraining order against him."

"Good. I'm coming over."

Leaving my room, I went to theirs and Nelly opened the door, quickly pulling me inside. The girls came to me and were clinging to me for dear life. I pulled Nelly to me and led them all to the bed. "Everything's gonna be okay. A'ight girls?"

Their whimpers and the tremble in their hands only pissed me off and they weren't my children. They only nodded their heads in response to what I'd said. "Do y'all like IHOP?"

They both quickly nodded and Zahria smiled slightly. "Okay. Then we're going there for breakfast."

They both stood from the bed and went to the sink to brush their teeth. I pulled Nelly in my arms as they looked at us through the mirror. At this point, I didn't care if they saw me being affectionate with Nelly. I was almost sure she didn't care, either. She didn't say a word, just laid against my chest. I kissed her head and said, "You okay?"

She shook her head. Grabbing her shoulders, I held her away from me and said, "I don't care what it looks like or what anybody has to say about it, but you're moving out of that house when y'all get back. Whether y'all move in with me or I help you to get an apartment, y'all are leaving. And when we get back to Beaumont, you need to file a restraining order. The hotel personnel can vouch for you. But I need to know that y'all are safe. And another thing, you need to call OnStar or whoever to get him off the permissions for that app. That's the only way I can think of that he found out where you were."

"The car is in both our names. The only way I could take him off is to provide legal documents stating that we were separated or divorced. I already called. As long as his name is on the car, he has a right to it. I've never been afraid of Broderick until now. He's never been forceful, other than with his words. Seeing how he scared our babies is making me more cautious now. How could he do this to our children?"

I swiped her tears with my thumb as I stared into her eyes. "I got'chu."

Leaning in and kissing her forehead, I then pulled her to me as the girls looked on. I gestured for them to come over with a tilt of my head. Tiana sat next to me and Zahria sat next to her mama, leaning against her. Nelly sat up and looked at her daughters. I stood so Tiana could get next to her mama. "Girls, I'm so sorry. I don't know what got into your daddy. I don't believe he would ever hurt one of us, but I have to be sure. His actions frightened me, and I know the two of you were scared also."

They both nodded as tears streamed down their faces. I admired Nelly for giving them the facts. She didn't try to sugar coat what was going on with their dad and their family as a unit. "Mommy, is Daddy going to jail?"

"No. But he had to leave us alone. It's against the law for him to harass us this way. Had he not left, he would have gone to jail. I'm not trying to keep y'all from your dad. I just want to have a peaceful weekend without all the arguing. You guys can see him when we get back tomorrow."

"I don't want to see him. He was mean to you and I don't like it," Tiana voiced.

"Me either, Mommy. We're gonna stay with you."

She hugged them tightly to her, then kissed their foreheads. I stood there silently for a few minutes, then said, "I'm gonna go back to my room to get dressed. That way I can take you ladies out for breakfast and just spend the entire day having a great time. Is that cool with y'all?"

They all nodded, and Nelly said, "Thank you, East, for being here for us."

"I wouldn't have it any other way. Be back in a few minutes."

Nelly nodded with a tight smile on her face as I turned to leave. When I walked out and the door closed, I leaned against it for a moment, taking deep breaths. It took a lot to restrain myself. That nigga was a bitch and the first time I got a moment with him face to face, I would let him know it. Those girls didn't deserve to see me lose it on their daddy, although they'd asked for my help. Pushing away from the door, I went to my room, prepared to show them a day of fun... no worries, no stress... just fun.

After getting dressed, I made my way back to them. When Nelly opened the door, she looked beautiful, but I also noticed she was sweating. "You okay, Nel?"

"I'm not sure. I feel nauseated and my head is spinning. My glucose levels may be low."

"Well, let's get you seated. Where's your machine?"

She pointed to the dresser and said, "In my purse."

Going to it, I hurriedly went back to her and watched her try to dig through it to find her machine. She looked to be fading, though, so I hurriedly found it and she talked me through setting it up. Once I'd gotten the lancet in the device and had gotten a strip inserted into her meter, I pricked her finger. The girls were anxiously looking on, waiting to see what was going on. After I'd squeezed the blood out of her finger and laid the strip in it, the machine only took a couple of seconds to register. "It's fifty-eight, Nel. Is that bad?"

"Yeah. It's too low."

Zahria ran to the fridge and got her Fanta Orange drink and

handed it to her mama. Nelly drank it quickly, then laid in the bed. "Just give it time to go up and we can leave, East."

I was frozen in place like I was in wet cement, not knowing what to do. "It's gonna be fine. It makes me feel weak and out of it... jittery and dizzy. That's how I knew something was wrong. I'd gotten too worked up."

I laid next to her as the girls watched and pulled her in my arms. Her heart was crying out for me and I was gonna come in and save it... no more questions asked.

CHAPTER 15

N elsondra

"I'M GOING TO ROGER'S AND GET SOMETHING TO EAT. YOU WANT me to bring you a potato?"

I took the phone from my ear and stared at my screen. The girls and I had gotten home from Houston around two o'clock Sunday afternoon. We'd had an amazing time the rest of our time there, without hearing a peep from Broderick. That Saturday after breakfast, we'd gone to a matinee at the movies, then the zoo. Surprisingly, I only had to sit a couple of times to rest my feet. It was more so my idea to even go to the zoo. Today, I was packing some things. East had found an apartment yesterday and this morning, I'd gone to put down a deposit. We would be moving the coming weekend.

I hadn't told Broderick yet, which was why he was calling me like all was well in paradise. I hated when he did that shit. There had been no apology and he just wanted to pretend like ain't shit happened between us... like I didn't almost call the police on his ass just two days ago. He was leaving work later than usual and he knew

I loved the potatoes from Roger's BBQ Barn. He was never interested in helping me control my diet. My restraint was damn near nonexistent already, but him bringing shit to my mind that I shouldn't have anyway, didn't help.

I stood from the bed to stretch, then said to him, "Broderick, I don't want a potato. I'm busy packing."

"Where you going now?"

"Away from you, nigga."

"Naw. We need to talk about that shit. You said you would stay in the house until we came to an agreement about the house. I ain't even signed no papers yet. You filed already?"

"My lawyer is working on the paperwork. So that's a yes."

He was quiet for a moment, then he said, "I'm on my way."

"No. I don't wanna talk to you. The only reason I answered the phone is because I thought you were calling about the girls. There is nothing more for us to talk about regarding our marriage. I'm done. I filed a restraining order on your ass anyway."

That muthafucka hung up in my face. I didn't even know if he'd heard my last line. "Girls!"

We had to get out of the house. I didn't want to be here to have to deal with him right now. If he was near Roger's, then we had ten minutes to get out of the house. "Ma'am?"

"Let's go!"

I quickly grabbed my purse and made my way to the door as they caught up with me. "Where are we going?" they asked, running toward me with their tablets in tote.

"Granny and Grampy's."

"Yay!"

I hurriedly locked the door and got to the car, moving a lot quicker than normal. Peeling out of the driveway, I took off toward their house, passing Broderick's truck down the street. I saw his brake lights in my rearview, then he turned around in one of our neighbor's driveway and followed us. "Mommy, why are you driving so fast?" Tiana asked.

"Was that Daddy?" Zahria asked.

"Yes."

"Mommy, call Mr. East. I'm scared."

Just the fact that they wanted me to call East saddened me. Broderick used to be their everything and now that they'd witnessed his mistreatment of me, they were afraid of him. I hated that. I never wanted my girls to be in fear of their own father. When I turned in my parents' driveway, I pulled under the awning, seeing their door was open. "Come on y'all."

They hurriedly got out of the car with me as Broderick turned in the driveway. The horrible part about this was that they would probably try to make us resolve our issues. When we walked in, the girls ran to the back. "Hey. What y'all doing here today? Thought y'all were coming tomorrow," my dad inquired.

I sat across from him as Broderick walked through the backdoor. My dad frowned slightly as he stared at me. He knew something was wrong. "You and Broderick arguing? Y'all need to just fix it."

How dare he fucking tell me to fix it and he didn't know what I was going through? That shit irritated me even more. My own dad... not worrying about why his daughter was pissed and running to their house for protection and solace... just saying to fix it. I slowly shook my head and chuckled, although wasn't shit funny. Broderick walked over to him and shook his hand. "What's up, Pops?"

"Hey, doc."

"Nel, come outside so we can talk."

"Hell no," I said, staring at him. "Where's Mama?" I asked my dad.

"She went to the store," my dad answered.

"Nel, please. Come outside. Where are the girls?"

"In the back."

"Since you won't go outside, I'll leave the room so y'all can talk," my daddy said, standing from his recliner.

I swallowed the lump in my throat as my daddy walked out of the room. As soon as he was out of earshot, Broderick said, "Why you gotta always make shit difficult? All you had to do was wait for me at the house, so I can talk to you there."

"Fuck you. I'm about to call the police. Like I said, I have a restraining order against you."

His eyes widened and he crossed the room, snatching my phone from my hand. The last thing I wanted to do was have him arrested, but he was going overboard. Standing from the couch, I went for my parents' house phone, but Broderick pushed me to my dad's recliner. "You ain't finna call no-fucking-body. I been trying to give you the benefit of the doubt, but I know that nigga was with y'all in Houston. I saw his punk ass walk out the hotel with y'all Saturday."

My eyes widened, then they suddenly narrowed. "I think you must be the punk ass. You obviously waited around for us to come out for a reason. When you saw him, you failed to make your presence known. Why? East intimidates you, doesn't he?"

"I ain't scared of that nigga. I didn't want my girls to witness me fucking him up. They seemed to be happy."

"Well, now, they're afraid of you. So, let that shit sink in."

He stood still as my phone slipped from his hands. When it did, he immediately went to the back as I hopped up from the recliner, picking up my phone from the floor as I ran after him. The girls were in my parents' bed and they were holding on to each other while he stood there trying to explain himself. "Don't y'all know that Daddy loves y'all? I would never hurt my babies," he explained as tears ran down his cheeks.

"Then why are you being so mean to Mommy?" Zahria asked.

"I'm not being mean—"

"Yes, you are!" Tiana yelled.

"What's going on?" a voice behind me asked.

I turned to see my mama standing there with my nephew. She'd gotten him from daycare. Broderick ran his hand down his face and left the room. "Sugar Bear, what's wrong?"

I rolled my eyes at her nickname for him. As I walked over to the bed to embrace my daughters, my mama asked, "What's going on, Nel?"

"We're divorcing."

"What? Why? What happened?"

"Too much to talk about in front of the girls. I'm tired, Ma. I've done everything I know to do to make him happy, but he's selfish, inconsiderate, and..."

"Mean!" Zahria yelled, then broke out in tears.

That shit broke me down, too. I couldn't take this. Being here, having to talk about what was going on between us only to be told that we needed to fix it would be a waste of my time, energy, and the mere effort. As I held her, my phone chimed. After wiping my tears, I pulled it from my pocket to see a text from East. *Hey, baby. How's your day going?*

I thought about how I'd kissed his lips and how good his embrace felt. Doing that in front of my girls didn't bother me one bit. I responded, *Hey. Like shit.*

My mama huffed loudly, then walked out of the room. I was almost sure that they were outside talking to Broderick and he was "pouring out his fucking heart," making them believe that everything was my fault. My mama was probably wiping away his tears as we spoke. My phone chimed again. *Meet me at my house. I'm about to go on my lunch break.*

"Come on, girls. Let's go see East."

They both hopped up from the bed, ready to leave. I didn't blame them. I was so ready to leave this bullshit, too. Had Broderick not followed us, I wouldn't have had to tell them what was going on at all. It would have been a normal visit. I'd gotten used to hiding my disappointments, fear, and heartache from them. I was tired of hiding. As I walked outside, just as I thought they were all sitting there talking as my sister drove up. Thankfully, he hadn't parked behind me. "Bye, y'all."

"Wait, Nel. Don't leave. Y'all need to talk."

"I'm so done talking. I been putting up with his bullshit for the past two years. I'm sick of it. Y'all love him that much, then adopt his ass."

The girls had run to the car, so I unlocked it, then started it. "Ask him why his daughters are afraid of him and why I have a restraining order on his ass." Turning to face Broderick, I said, "Next time you come near me, I *will* call the police. No questions asked."

I hopped in the car and left as my sister waved, a look of confusion adorning her face. Glancing back at my girls, I asked, "Y'all okay?"

"Yes, ma'am."

"I understand y'all are afraid, but for what it's worth, I don't believe your dad would lay a finger on either of you. He loves y'all. I know that to be true. I don't want y'all to be afraid in his presence. For whatever reason, he just can't seem to love me. That's why we're getting a divorce. I don't want you guys to feel like he hates y'all, because he doesn't. Okay?"

"Yes, ma'am," they said in unison.

When we got to East's house, he was in the driveway waiting on us. I was so tired of this game. I didn't like East being in the middle of my drama, especially since I couldn't proceed with him the way he really wanted. Taking a deep breath, I got out of the car, only to see another one drive up. He frowned as the girls and I made our way to him. It was the chick from the party. "Girls, get back in the car."

"Aww, but Mo—"

"Now," I said sternly.

"Where y'all going, Nelly?"

"Hey, Easton," his lady friend said.

"What are you doing here, Whitney?"

"We need to talk."

I walked away, my feet practically crippling me. I'd had enough drama for the day, and I knew for a fact that I couldn't handle any more. "Nel! Don't leave."

I couldn't even turn around to look at him. My heart was in my feet and I was walking all over it. This was proof that I needed to be alone. Grabbing my phone, I called the apartment complex to see when would be the earliest I could move in and they'd informed me that I could move whenever I wanted to. Backing out of the driveway as East argued with the beautiful woman in his driveway, I shut my heart off to love. *I'd fallen for East.* He'd expressed his love for me, and I had no doubt that he was sincere, but it was best that I was alone for now.

Sitting at the traffic light by his house, I decided to drive to a nearby park and let the girls get out and burn off some energy. I knew they were mentally drained with the happenings of the last hour because I was, too. Surprisingly, they hadn't asked any questions. While they played, I searched for moving companies. After finding one that seemed reputable, I called and hired them. They assured me that they would be there to start packing and moving things tomorrow. I sat back on the bench, listening to my phone ring. Seeing East's number only made my heart ache for him.

For his touch.

His loving words.

The solace I found in his embrace.

It was then that I realized I would have to be all that for my-damn-self. Depending on him for my comfort and happiness was wrong. I needed to find happiness within and with my children before I could seek it elsewhere. *God, please help me. I need you.* The tears cascaded down my cheeks as a lady stopped her run. "Ma'am, are you okay?"

"Yes, ma'am. I will be."

She nodded and smiled tightly, then continued her run. This purge was necessary, and I should have done it a lot sooner. The hurt had only gotten worse by hiding it and ignoring it all this time. Regardless of my health issues, I deserved better. I deserved for someone to love me for more than what I could do for them. But first, I needed to fall in love with me all over again. I couldn't expect anyone else to love me if I didn't love myself. And lately, when I looked in the mirror, I didn't feel love. I needed to get that back.

When I stood from the bench, the girls ran over to me. I hugged them and hobbled my way to the car. I needed to go home and lie down. After going to the apartment complex to get the key and taking a shower, I would do just that and wait for the beginning of my new life to begin. We'd taken the ten-minute drive to the complex and I went inside to sign more paperwork as the girls looked around. I'd requested a downstairs unit and thankfully, they had one available. Once I'd gotten the key to our two-bedroom apartment and we were walking back to the car, Tiana asked, "Is this where we will be living now?"

"Yeah. You like it?"

"I like the pool!" Zahria said.

"I do, too. But as long as we're with you, Mommy, I don't care where we live."

I put my arm around my baby, knowing that we would be just fine. God would take care of us and he would give me the strength to come out on top.

CHAPTER 16

E aston

MY PICTURE HAD TO BE IN THE DICTIONARY NEXT TO THE WORD rage because that was all I felt while I argued with Whitney's ass, watching Nelly drive away. Proving that I was there for her and her beautiful girls was my main priority and Whitney had fucked that up. It made it seem like my personal business wasn't intact. Seeing her haul ass, I could tell she was hurt and that she wasn't feeling her best physically, either. She had a slight limp as she walked back to the car. That was an entire month ago.

I felt like I was going insane without her. She was all I could think about and I missed her so much. Nothing in my life was the same with her missing. Even shit she had nothing to do with was affected. My mama had been singing her 'I told you so' tune and had tried to introduce me to a lady at her church. I could only roll my eyes and stay to myself mostly so I wouldn't have to deal with her shenanigans. I didn't have time to fool around with her.

Every time I thought about Nelly, I thought about what Whitney did to fuck with her. Her ass didn't want anything that day but to start shit. She saw Nelly turning to come to my house. I never took her as the type to be with stupid bullshit. She was jealous of Nel and the relationship she had with me. If she was a man, I would have knocked her ass out. Her exact words were, *Now, you'll see what it feels like to waste your time.*

I'd been calling Nelly every day for the past month and sending messages. That bullshit was bothering the hell out of me. I hated when she went ghost on me. That shit was immature and selfish. As soon as I thought that, my thoughts shifted. Maybe I was the one that was selfish. Nelly was going through life-changing events and all I could think about was how miserable *I* was. But I did want to help her through it... help the girls through it.

Leaving work, I made my way home. My routine had been simple. I went to work five days a week, went to my mother's house once a week, and to the gym four times a week. Other than that, I was at home, according to my mama, sinking in depression. I'd gone by Nelly's parents' house a couple of times, checking on her. The first time, they hadn't heard from her either and were extremely worried about her. The second time, they'd said she was doing okay, but had told them that she didn't want to be bothered with anyone.

After that, I chose to just call her every day, hoping that one day she would answer my call. I'd already made a phone call today and as usual, she didn't answer. My mama was right. I was depressed. My mood was always fucked, and it didn't take much for me to snap. Anybody could get it, especially my coworkers. I took my frustrations with customers out on everybody else. So, I needed to get it together quickly before I lost my job. Ain't no way I'd be able to afford that.

However, when I got home, Nelly's car was in the driveway. I damn near jumped out the car and let it keep rolling. That was just how excited I was to see that car. Without going inside the garage, I put the car in park and hopped out as she got out of her vehicle. She smiled slightly as I approached her. "Nelly... damn," I said as my chest heaved.

I didn't want to show too much excitement because I didn't

know why she was here. When I got a couple of feet from her, I stopped. She smiled and said, "It's like that, nigga?"

I smiled back and rushed her, holding her tightly in my arms. "Come on in, big head."

As I unlocked the door, she wrapped her arms around my waist and laid her head on my back. I was a big nigga, tough as hell, but that very action caused a lump to form in my throat. Moving forward, pulling away from her, I walked inside, and she followed me. After I closed the door, I sat at the bar, then looked at her and said, "I was so damn worried about you. Where you been?"

"I needed time away from everybody. My well-being was being based on a lot of other people's needs and opinions instead of my own. I'm sorry that I ghosted you for all this time, but I was able to come to terms with a lot of things and redirect my energy into things that mattered, like starting over and taking care of my children, making sure they understood what was going on. Do you forgive me?"

I sat there with a frown on my face while she talked, and I could tell that made her nervous. Honestly, I was upset that she shut me out. I could have been there to help her through the changes. That was all I wanted. She could have at least replied to my text messages. My frown deepened as I stared at her. "I'm not gon' lie, Nelly, but that makes me feel a way. Wasn't I worth a text back? Even if it was just you saying that you needed space and that you and the kids were okay? Man, I been walking around here stressed and snapping on people because I was worried about you. How was that shit fair to me?"

Her face reddened as I stood and paced in front of her. I loved Nel and everything in me wanted to just forgive her and move on from here. Feeling her arms wrapped around me was something I'd been desperately craving for the past month. I stopped pacing and stared at her, then wiped my hand down my face, trying to find the right words to say. As I did, she stood from the barstool and got right in my face. Putting her hands to my cheeks, she pulled my face to hers and kissed me tenderly. "I'm sorry, East. I love you."

Claiming my mouth again, she slid her tongue inside and I

couldn't help but grip her ass as her tongue soothed my mental and tamed my nerves. It was like the anger melted away upon contact and I felt like she knew that. Slowly pulling away from her, I stared in her eyes for a moment. "I love you, too. That's why I'm tripping about your silence, because you know I was there for you, whatever you needed."

Sitting back on the barstool, she looked away for a moment, then frowned slightly. "Me not responding had everything to do with me... not you. I needed to be sure that I was doing what was right for me and my babies. I didn't want to base my final decision on how I felt for you. You're perfect, East. You always have been. But you've been perfect as my friend. Transitioning into more has me nervous as hell. Broderick was my husband... the man I spent almost twenty years of my life with, damn near sixteen years married. He's the father of my children. There was so much to lose. I needed to be alone to repro-gram my thinking and realize that by leaving him, there was so much to gain."

She stood from her stool and grabbed her keys. "I expected you to understand that I had a lot of shit going on. But maybe I was wrong. I apologize for wasting your time."

"Naw... put those keys down. You ain't finna run off. We gon' finish talking about this and come to a resolution. I knew you had shit going on. I was there for some of it. So, I expected *you* to under-stand and realize that I was there for you as a friend. I needed you to see that I would do whatever for you and those girls. But it's cool. It's cool that I damn near worried myself to death about you. You didn't even have the decency to even say, *fuck off.* I would have respected that more than your silence, Nelsondra."

Her eyebrows lifted slightly. I never called her Nelsondra. I understood that she needed time to herself, but how hard would it have been for her to communicate that to me? "So, I suppose you have your issues with Whitney handled then. I figured she was keeping you pretty busy anyway. I just left a hurtful and abusive rela-tionship. I wasn't up for no bullshit. I'm not trying to put my girls through any unnecessary changes! Why can't you understand that shit? I'm tired of arguing... I'm tired of having to explain myself. I just wanna live! I wanna enjoy life without the bullshit of wondering how someone else feels about me."

The tears had fallen down her face as she yelled at me. The heat rushed to my face and I yelled right back. "Just because you were hurting, don't give you a right to hurt somebody else! You know I wasn't involved with Whitney like that. She was trying to start shit and that was exactly what she did. You know me, Nel. You know I would never lead you on or bullshit you. I can't take this running in and out of my life. Real shit. Either you gon' let me be there or not. Yo' choice."

I didn't mean to go as far as giving her an ultimatum, but that was how I felt. The back and forth was on my nerves. I knew her feelings for that nigga were going haywire, but what did that shit have to do with me? She knew where we stood. Even if she didn't want the relationship, she knew where I stood as her friend. It almost seemed as if that twenty-year absence should have been longer. She grabbed her keys once again, and I knew I had to do something. She wasn't leaving me again without effort from me. "Bye, East."

I swiftly pulled her to me and felt the tremble course through her body. Although Nel was tall, I was taller, and I towered over her... a good eight inches taller than her. "You willing to just walk out on me, Nelly? Leave me standing here because of what you went through?"

She lowered her head, but I lifted it by placing my fingers under her chin. "Naw. Look at me and tell me you wanna leave. Tell me to go fuck myself instead of your fat pussy, Nel. Tell me you can do without my touch."

I slid my fingers down the side of her face. It was like she'd stopped breathing. Leaning over, I kissed her neck, then whispered in her ear, "Tell me to stop, Nel."

Her hands went to my head and pulled it up to hers. Staring into her eyes, I knew what she needed. Our needs were one and the same. I decided to just take her as she was. She was here now, and I didn't want to lose her again. Grabbing her hand, I led her to my bedroom. Before I could turn around, she pulled me to her, kissing me like her life depended on it. Yanking my shirt, I could hear it tearing, but I didn't give a fuck. She quickly unbuckled my belt and unbuttoned my pants, pulling them down, then my drawers. My dick bounced out of my shit, ready for action.

I pulled her shirt off and unfastened her bra, then she shimmied her way out of her pants and underwear. She immediately went to my bed and got on all fours. "I need you, East," she moaned. "I missed you so much."

Looking at the juices leaking from her, I knew that shit was probably true. My dick twitched in response. There wasn't a condom in sight, but I couldn't resist that shit. Kicking my pants and underwear off my feet, I let my dick lead me right to her. Pushing inside of her put us both out of our misery. Nothing else mattered at this point. Watching her cream coat my dick caused me to groan. "Fuck, Nel. Tell me you here to stay, baby. Shit."

"I ain't going nowhere, baby. Fuck me, please."

Slapping her ass, then grabbing it, I thrust into her forcefully and gave her just what she asked for as she came all over my dick. "I can't believe you was gon' leave this shit behind, girl. All this history, chemistry, and love."

I continued pounding into her as she screamed out her pleasure, sucking my soul out of me with every thrust. Her ass jiggled against me and I couldn't help but grab a handful of it. Slowing my pace, I pulled out of her and went to my knees on the floor and sucked her pussy from the back. Indulging in her flavor had been on my mind since the last time I tasted her. That shit was like voodoo, calling out to me every time I was near her. Sliding my arms between her legs and circling them around her waist, I pulled her to me as I teased her trigger, begging her to shoot.

I could feel her trembles against my face, and I knew she was about to bless me. I quickly stood and shoved my dick back in her pussy and dropped spit to her ass, pushing my finger inside. She immediately came. "East! Fuck! Oh my God!"

"Yeah, Nel. This shit is so good. You can't leave me again. Bring my babies to me. Let me take care of y'all."

She turned to look at me and I could see the tears falling from her eyes. That wasn't just sex talk. I wanted them in my life... no, I needed them in my life. *Family.* It was something I knew I wanted. It didn't matter whether she had kids already. Just the little time I'd spent around them, I'd fallen in love with them as well. Slowing my pace again, I could feel that my dick was on the brink of causing a major disaster, but I wasn't ready to end the session. Truthfully, I didn't know what Nel would do after this. While she'd said that she wouldn't leave, I just didn't know. Leaning over her, I whispered, "I love you so much, Nel."

Her cries stopped me because I didn't know what the issue was. "Please, don't stop, East. Please. Don't. Stop."

I started stroking her again slowly, then leaned over and kissed her back several times. Asking her why she was crying came to mind, but I didn't want to ruin the moment. So instead, I asked, "Can I cum inside you, baby?"

"Yeah... oh, God... please..."

Before I could bust, she came once again, nearly collapsing to the bed. I followed her ass, though, and bust one of my own. She'd zapped the little bit of energy I had left. I could lay on her and go right to sleep at this point. Knowing that I was the only man that had made her cum during sex had puffed my chest out. Had a nigga feeling like Big Willie and shit. I kissed her back and stood, doing my best to watch her feet. We were both quiet. I supposed neither of us knew what to say.

Letting my thoughts marinate in my mind, I went to the bathroom and washed up, then got a towel to clean her with. When I went back into the room, she was lying on her back, her legs agape. I wanted to dive right back between them, but I knew we definitely needed to talk. Taking the towel from me, she held it between her legs as she moaned. Tucking my bottom lip in my mouth, I shook my head slowly. *This shit had to work.*

CHAPTER 17

N elsondra

WHAT I'D EXPERIENCED WITH EAST HAD TO BE LOVEMAKING. Broderick had never been able to accomplish the things East had my body feeling. I supposed if he took a moment to think about me and my enjoyment versus getting his next nut, things would have been different. He'd finally accepted that I was done with his ass. As I wiped myself, I knew East needed conversation... an explanation of where things were going with us and what had gone on between me and Broderick. After sitting up in the bed, I handed him the towel and he threw it to the restroom floor, then laid next to me. "I know I owe you more of an explanation... of what was going on."

Pulling me to him, he remained quiet as he stared at me. So, I continued, "When I came to your house with the girls, I was running from Broderick. I was packing our things, getting ready for our move. He called and threatened to come over, so the girls and I left and went to my parents. Of course, he saw us and followed us there. My parents were trying to make me sit and talk to him and I'd had enough. When I showed up here, you were my last resort. I didn't want to go home because I didn't want to deal with him."

"Why didn't you call the police? You have a restraining order."

"Because the last thing I wanna do is have my children's dad arrested in front of them. Especially if he isn't threatening me with bodily harm. When I left from here, I took them to the park, and I sat there and thought about the way my life was going. I was tired, East, and I knew that I had to do better for my children. They were so scared. They wanted me to call you. But instead, after leaving the park, I went to the apartment complex and picked up the key. I called a moving company to get us moved."

Taking a deep breath, I closed my eyes, trying not to let my emotions overtake me. "When I got home, he was waiting on us. We argued about bullshit... the same shit we've been arguing about for the past two years. All the reasons why I want to leave and why I think we can't work the shit out. I cursed so much in front of my children... screamed and cried. I know they were scared, but I couldn't be there for them in that moment. Because I couldn't, I felt like less of a mother... less of a woman. I hated that I felt I drug you into all of my shit and that night after he left, I promised myself that I would get myself together before I contacted you again."

"Nel—"

Cutting him off, I continued, "No. I had to do that for me. I was broken. I'm not completely healed from it now, but I'm not like I was that night. My extremities, including my arms, were hurting so bad and my blood pressure and glucose levels were through the roof. I was seeing double. He left me there like that, knowing that I could barely walk. Instead, he threw a pity party for himself with my children. Apologizing to them for scaring them and how he just didn't want to lose them. He made it seem like I was the villain to my children, like I was standing in the way of us being a family."

I swiped the tears that had fallen as East stared at me. Rehashing all that shit was hurtful as hell but once I got through it, I would never have to bring it up again. Burying myself even more in his embrace, I inhaled deeply and released it. "The very next day, we moved. We started counseling. I go once a week alone and the kids go once a week as well. I don't want them to suffer from this turmoil. They are still young, but not young enough to where they would forget. They could carry those memories with them for the rest of their lives."

"I'm so sorry you felt like you had to go through that alone, Nel." He kissed my forehead, then asked, "So, what's next?"

"We've already had an arbitration. After that day, he only called me to see the kids. Once I moved, he didn't know where I'd gone. I'd called OnStar and had the vehicle locate feature temporarily disabled. So, in order to see them, he had to humble himself. We met at neutral grounds and for two weeks I wouldn't allow him to take them out of my sight. In arbitration, we settled everything. There was no need in going to court since we agreed on everything. The house is up for sale and he gets the kids every other weekend. It was agreed that if he wanted them more often, he'd call. My parents were there whenever I called them, and they promised to keep their two cents to themselves."

I chuckled slightly, remembering the conversation with them and how they were quick to agree so they could see their grandkids. "So, are you telling me that you're mine now?"

"I'm telling you, that I'm here. I wanna take things slow, but I already know that's not going to happen. Judging by what happened a little while ago, I know that I won't be able to resist you anymore. But as far as us openly being a couple, I wanna keep that under wraps for a little bit... just until the ink dries on the divorce papers."

Sliding his hands to my ass, he asked, "So how's your health now?"

"Oh, things are so much better. My blood pressure is under control. I started going to a chiropractor and because I sit at home on the computer all day, my neck was severely strained. Believe it or not, me going has relieved my leg pain and some of my foot pain. My lower back was out of whack, too."

"Wow. That's good, Nel. What about your sugar?"

"It's still a little crazy, but I'm working on it. I've been eating better, but the hardest part is trying to get the girls to eat better. Tiana is so stubborn. She'll starve before she eats certain things."

"Damn, I'm glad you're here, but I guess I need to let you up so you can get ready to go."

"If you're cool with it, I'd like to stay here. The girls are at my parents' house tonight. So, I don't have to rush home. It's not like I have anybody to go home to an—"

His lips crashed into mine and I couldn't help but bring my hands to his face. That month without him had been rough as hell, but I didn't need to involve him in any more of the drama from the three-ring circus Broderick had put me through. It took Whitney showing up that day for me to realize I was being selfish... the very thing I accused Broderick of being. East was a good man and I was taking advantage of his love and his affection. I listened to women say all the time about what they would do if they were in a situation like mine. I was one of those women at one time. No one knew what they would do in a situation until they were in it. I never would have thought I would have cheated on Broderick, but I did. Regardless of how broken and neglected I was, or how unloved I felt, I was still married. It was wrong,

Just like I was technically still married now. The divorce hadn't been finalized yet. But I couldn't go another day without East. I knew I still had a long way to go, but now that Broderick's ass wasn't damn near stalking me everywhere I went, I felt a sense of freedom. That restraining order was still in place though, just in case. When East pulled away from me, he said, "Let's go take a shower."

I smiled slightly. This would be the relationship I'd been craving. I hated that Broderick couldn't give me that because it was truly how we started. Things had been rough at times along the way, but the past two years, it was like he was a different person and he didn't know how to come back from himself. Following East to the shower, I released a deep breath and prayed that things would never change between us. Even after fifteen, almost sixteen, years of marriage to Broderick, I was still willing to find love. The fact that that love would be with East, someone who'd always been good to me, was the icing on the cake.

IT HAD BEEN TWO WEEKS AND THINGS BETWEEN EAST AND I HAD been so relaxed, it was like we'd never spent time apart. We were in my apartment, cooking together and dancing while the girls laughed. "What dance is that?" Tiana asked while laughing.

"It's the cabbage patch, girl! You need to learn your dance history," East joked.

"The cabbage patch?" she questioned, her thick eyebrows to the sky, as she continued to laugh.

Zahria had fallen over to the sofa she was laughing so hard. I'd gotten the divorce decree a couple of days ago and I knew that was a symbol of the end, but also one of a new beginning. East and I had been spending time together almost every day. If the girls and I weren't at his house, he was at our place. The girls had gotten comfortable with him around and they'd mended their relationship with their dad. They actually looked forward to spending time with him, even when it wasn't his weekend.

I realized that all the times I'd threatened to leave Broderick may have been the reason why he didn't take me seriously this last time, but whatever the case, I was glad that he finally realized there wasn't a thing he could do to keep me somewhere I no longer wanted to be. It was almost like he completely gave up after that last argument. He began focusing more on his duties as a father and making sure the girls were good. While I knew he would take care of them, I filed for child support anyway. I had to be sure that the two of them would be taken care of, no matter what.

As we finished cooking the mashed potatoes and green beans to go along with the meatloaf, East pulled me to him from behind and kissed my neck. "Baby, why don't you go rest your feet? I'll fix plates and Tiana and Zahria can get our drinks."

He kissed my lips and led me to the table while the girls went to wash their hands for dinner. "I actually feel fine, East. I'm not in any pain today."

"Well, save that extra energy for tonight once the girls leave for their dad's house."

I was somewhat nervous about that. Today would be the first time that East would be here when Broderick came to get the girls. I was praying that Broderick would act like he had a little sense. The divorce was final and there wasn't shit he could do to prevent that, simply because he was bitter or jealous. Despite the bullshit, he knew me. Had he not been such a jackass to me, there would have been no room for East to come in and sweep me off my feet. As East was about to walk away, I pulled him back by his hand. "Thank you, baby. I got'chu."

He gave me one of those evil-looking grins that he was so good at giving, making my sex enlarge her territory to accept his massive dick. Broderick was a nice size but when I first felt East's dick, it caught me by surprise. Being as tall as he was, he fulfilled the validity of the stereotype. He knew what it meant when I said that, though. I'd been able to ride him a couple of times. I could count how many times I felt good enough to do that since I'd been diagnosed. It seemed being with East was good for my health as well as my spirit. "Mommy, do you want water to drink?"

"Yes, please. Thank you, baby."

East began bringing plates to the table and they all joined me. We held hands and East blessed the food, then said, "I put my pinky toe in those mashed potatoes."

Tiana and Zahria's faces scrunched up in disgust as I laughed. "That means they're really good. It's only an expression that mainly older people used to say just how good something is."

"Oh. Well, they shouldn't say it like that. It makes me not wanna eat it. Mr. East that's nasty."

East and I laughed again and continued eating. The mashed potatoes were extremely good though, so he didn't lie about that. As we continued to eat, East said, "Oh! I forgot I bought y'all gifts. I'll be right back."

He stood from the table and I knew he wanted to give them their gifts before Broderick got here. Otherwise, he would have finished eating first. He always bought them little surprises and I thought that was sweet of him. Almost every day for the past two weeks, he'd come bearing gifts. The girls had excited expressions on their faces as they ate and Zahria asked Tiana, "What do you think he got us?"

"I don't know, but I hope he got me something to do with unicorns."

I rolled my eyes slightly as Tiana exclaimed, "I saw that!"

"And?" I said back as I chuckled. "I'm supposed to be scared?"

"Yep!" she exclaimed, then laughed as I shook my head and rolled my eyes again.

She was definitely my mini-me, always thinking she was running something. When East walked back in with gift bags, I got somewhat excited. It was rare that I experienced surprises like this. He handed the gifts to the girls as they giggled in excitement. As they rummaged through their bags, they both started screaming. I winced at the high-pitched screams and East pressed his finger to one ear with one eye closed.

They began jumping around showing each other their gifts. Zahria held roller skates in her hand and Tiana had LED lights that she'd been wanting to string along her side of their room. "Thank you, Mr. East!"

They hugged him one at a time, then went back to their gifts as East handed me a bag. "And this is for you, baby. I hope you like them."

I smiled at him, knowing that whatever it was, it was extremely thoughtful of him to think about me. Opening the bag, it was full of oils and lotions from bath and body. At the bottom was a pair of furry house shoes. I looked up at him and smiled. "Wow. Thank you so much."

"You never buy anything for yourself and I want that to change, baby. I know the girls are your main priority, but I want you to also focus on you. From now on, one day every other week, you'll be getting gentle massages to help with your circulation. You sit a lot for work, and I need you to stay at your best. You can't take care of them unless you take care of you."

Those gifts were more for him to use on me. He was still rubbing my legs and feet down every day. It was how we wound down and got ready for the night's activities once the girls went to sleep. I kissed his lips and before I could express my gratitude, the doorbell rang. *Broderick.* "You want me to go to the back?"

"No. Stay. I no longer care about his perception of me or anyone else's. Okay?"

He nodded, then smiled as I went to the door. The girls hurried to get their overnight bags, then came back and brought their plates to the kitchen sink. When I opened the door, Broderick said, "Hey, Nel."

"Hey. The girls are ready," I said as I opened the door wider, allowing him to walk in.

When he saw East, he turned slightly red but nodded his head. East did the same as the girls rushed him. "Hey, Daddy's babies. I missed y'all."

"Missed you, too, Daddy!" Zahria said.

"Well, tell your mom and Easton bye, so we can go."

The girls hugged me tightly and I was relieved at how smoothly things had gone. Broderick was trying to act like it didn't bother him to see Easton there, but I knew it did. However, I believed he was finally accepting responsibility for the role he played in my departure from our marriage. I was emotionally gone a long time ago... long before I got the nerve to physically leave. Once they hugged East and thanked him for the gifts again, Broderick said, "I'll have them back tomorrow night. I have to work Sunday."

"Okay," I said as I nodded, then followed them to the door.

When they walked through the door, I saw him glance at East as he cleaned up the table. *Yeah, muthafucka. The small things mattered.* Whenever we were done with dinner when I was married to him, he would leave his plate right there on the table like he had a servant. *He did, bitch. You were his servant.* As I watched them leave, East stood by my side and wrapped his arm around my waist. He kissed my cheek as Broderick took one last look, then got in his truck. I closed the door and said, "That went better than I thought it would."

"A lot better than I thought it would, too. Our last face to face wasn't good."

"I know. But thankfully, he realizes what we had is a done deal."

"Well, come on. Let me get this body washed up and oiled down so you can lube me up with some of that natural oil."

Bringing my hands to his face, I pulled him to me and kissed his lips. "I love you, East and I'm glad you didn't give up on me."

"Girl, you my A-one since day one. I would have never given up on you."

"But I mean as far as trying to pursue a relationship with me. This is the happiest I've been in a long time. I'm grateful that you friend requested me on Facebook."

He chuckled, then said, "Yeah, me too. I'm glad I was here for you when you needed me. I have to admit, I was damn near at my wits end on the relationship. But I'm glad I didn't throw in the towel on that. These last two weeks have been what I've been longing for my entire life... loving a woman with everything in me without having to wait until next lifetime."

EPILOGUE

E aston
    Six months later...

THE DOORBELL RANG, SO I WENT TO IT. NELLY WAS IN THE shower because we were going somewhere special tonight. Broderick was coming to get the girls. He and I were seeming to get along okay. We had yet to hold a conversation because there was really no need to. He and Nel had been doing well co-parenting. He always got the girls one night of the off weekend. Next weekend would be his designated time with them. He was a good father and I could respect him for that. Those little girls meant the world to him. When I opened the door, we shook hands and I invited him inside. "You wanna get the girls?" I asked him.

"Before I do, I just wanted to say thanks for being a respectable man around my daughters. They talk about you all the time."

I nodded. "I don't know any other way to be, man."

He looked down for a moment, then said, "Thank you for being good to Nelly. I fucked us up... bad. She deserves the world and I thought I'd given her that, but I couldn't seem to handle her illness the way I should have. In that respect, it was like I took the world back from her. She found what she was lacking with me, in you. While I hated losing her, I realize that I pushed her away. So, again, thank you for being what she needed."

My eyebrows had risen and stayed that way the entire time he was talking. This was the same dude that hit me in the jaw and that I damn near choked out on my front lawn. I didn't know what to say to what he said, so I nodded. "Umm... I should tell you that I plan to ask for her and the girls to move in with me, so she won't have to continue to pay rent. I wanted to ask her and let her talk to you about it, but since we're here, I thought I should mention it."

He nodded. "I trust you with my daughters. You haven't given me a reason not to. "

I extended my hand and he shook it as Zahria came running down the hallway. "Daddy!"

She jumped in his arms and he grunted like she was too heavy, causing her to giggle. Tiana came from the back with her overnight bag and said, "Z, go get your bag."

Zahria took off back to the room as Broderick said, "Go tell your mom we're about to leave."

"Okay."

We both stood there quietly waiting for them to return, which was only for a minute or so. They both hugged me, and Broderick and I shook hands again before they left. I sat on the couch, prepared to take my woman for a night out on the town. She'd been doing well with her diabetes and she'd lost fifteen pounds. The depression and stress of the divorce had caused her to gain a few pounds. She'd been going to the gym, working out on a stationary bicycle where she could sit for back support, a recumbent bike, and not have a lot of impact on her feet, like walking on a treadmill. I was proud of her for taking her health seriously. Because of her dedication, she was feeling so much better. But I wasn't crazy. I knew that she wasn't getting the support she needed before.

I refuse to eat anything she shouldn't have in front of her. While it was okay for her to cheat every now and then, she had to work harder to get her sugar to go back down to where it should be. Her

A1C levels were at a ten when I first went to the doctor with her. That was extremely high. It was no wonder her feet were hurting as badly as they were. So, I started educating myself on diabetes and how it affects the body. I knew she would need all the support she could get.

What I learned about Nelly was that most times she was good without sweets, alcohol, and fried foods. She only really wanted those things when someone else brought them up. The girls and I agreed that they wouldn't talk about those things in front of their mom until she was at a point in her lifestyle change where she could handle it. At her appointment two weeks ago, her A1C was now at a six point four. That was amazing, considering where she was six months ago. Her doctor was beyond pleased.

I asked her if it would be okay for Nelly to have a glass of wine this weekend and she said that she could as long as she didn't have dessert. We had reservations at The Grill, and I planned to ask her while we were there. As I sat on the couch in my white slacks, white shirt, and baby blue blazer, I checked the time to see we were on schedule. I'd accented my ensemble with some navy blue, suede loafers. I was clean as hell, if I had to say so myself. As I was about to turn on the TV, Nelly came out in a tan and navy blue dress that hugged her every curve. It was somewhat see-through, showing off her blue bra beneath it.

I hoped I wouldn't have to put nobody in their place because I would without hesitation. I stood from the couch as I scanned her body from her slicked ponytail to the boots she wore. *Boots!* "Nel... you're wearing heels. And a shoe that squeezes your foot."

"I know. I could actually get it on without wincing."

"Baby, that's amazing. And you look gorgeous. Damn..."

"Thank you, East. You look fine as hell. To the point where I just wanna undress all this thickness."

She came close to me and rubbed her hands up my chest and around my neck. I leaned over and kissed her cheek, then said, "Let's go. I'm starving."

"Me too."

I helped her into the car, and we took the ten-minute drive to

The Grill. We talked about the girls on the ride over and as I parked, she asked, "Broderick was cordial?"

"Yeah. He actually thanked me for taking care of your needs."

She frowned and said, "Nigga, whet?"

"Shocked the shit out of me, too."

I chuckled and got out of the car, then walked to her side to open her door and assist her out of the car. Licking my lips as I scanned her body, I said, "I don't know what possessed you to wear this, but I ain't gon' be able to concentrate on shit else."

"Good."

She nudged me with her shoulder as I held my arm out for her to wrap hers around and walked to the entrance. Once we were seated at a table clad with a red tablecloth, I pulled out a red cushioned seat for her to sit on. I didn't want to wait until the dinner was over before I asked her. I didn't have that much patience. After we ordered our drinks and an appetizer, I reached across the table and grabbed Nelly's hands. "This date was way overdue. Work has been crazy."

"It was definitely overdue, but I understood. Y'all have had so many promotions running lately, people are knocking each other down to get to those deals."

I smiled at her as the waitress set our drinks on the table. After nodding at her, expressing my thanks, I took a sip of my wine. My nerves were getting the best of me because I wasn't one hundred percent sure of what Nelly's response would be. However, I wanted to ask her before she renewed her lease. Once the waitress came back with our appetizer of crab cakes, I grabbed her hand and blessed the food.

After consuming a few bites, I knew it was time to proposition her. Standing from my chair and going to my knee in front of her, she nearly choked. I reached in my jacket pocket and pulled out a box that contained a three-carat diamond. "Nelly, you know I love you. Because of my love for you, I fell in love with Tiana and Zahria. There is nothing more that I want than for us to be together as a family. You know I'm not all that eloquent with words, but I know

Check Out Receipt

Perry Hall Branch
410-887-5195
www.bcpl.info

Wednesday, February 17, 2021 1:07:38 PM
35160

Item: 31183202335334
Title: Next lifetime
Call no.: Fiction WAL
Due: 03/10/2021

Total items: 1

You just saved $16.99 by using your
library today.

My Librarian
A one-on-one appointment for
personalized assistance with apps, eBooks,
job searches, writing resumes, email setup and m
ore.
Ask a staff member or check bcpl.info for detail
s.

that I don't want to ever let you go. So, I need to know if you will make me a happy man and be my wife."

Her hand went to her mouth as the tears slid down her cheeks. Her face had reddened, and I just hoped me being on my knee in these white pants wasn't in vain. I opened the box and her eyes widened even more so. "I want us to live under one roof as a family. Please don't leave me hanging, Nel. Tell me that you wanna make this official as bad as me."

"I-I'm sorry..."

I lowered my head. She was 'bout to shut me down in front of all the people watching. She pulled my face to hers and said, "I'm sorry for taking so long to say yes."

A slow smile crept on my lips and I immediately stood, pulling her from her seat. The people in the vicinity clapped as I slid the ring on her finger, then kissed her lips. She sat in her chair, staring at the ring, then looking up at me as I sat. "I'm so in shock, East. This ring is beautiful."

"I was hoping you weren't going to turn me down. You had me nervous for a minute."

"I could never turn you down again. You've been everything to me and the girls and we love you."

"You can take as much time as you need to pick a date to get married, but I wanna move you and the girls in with me."

"Wow, East. I was supposed to sign the lease on Monday."

"I know. That's why I knew I had to ask you now. I'm so happy that after everything you've been through, it didn't ruin your heart. I'm grateful that you were still willing to take a chance on love."

She smiled at me as I kissed her hand. I'd finally found my forever and she'd been in my life all along. Despite her marriage, I knew that she was the one for me and I was beyond thankful that I got to experience her this lifetime instead of next.

THE END

AFTERWORD

From the Author...

This book was so hard to write because it contained so much of me. I am a diabetic and have been for almost twenty years. I was also diagnosed with neuropathy two years ago and recently high blood pressure and fluid retention. A lot of Nel's feelings and emotions were my own. I cried through most of this book, but it was so therapeutic for me. There are times when my emotions are going haywire and I don't have a clue why. This book was my way of getting those feelings out, and I chose to share some of my personal experiences with you. So hopefully, I won't get any comments saying this book was unrealistic. LOL However, I hope you enjoyed reading about Nel's triumph and East's love for her. While that part was fictional, it was best for her situation.

There's also an amazing playlist on Apple Music and Spotify for this book under the same title that includes some great R&B tracks to tickle your fancy. Please keep up with me on Facebook (@authormonicawalters), Instagram (@authormonicawalters) and Twitter (@monlwalters). You can also visit my Amazon author page at www.amazon.com/author/monica.walters to view my releases. Please subscribe to my webpage for updates! https://authormonicawalters.com.

For live discussions, giveaways, and inside information on upcoming releases, join my Facebook group, Monica's Romantic Sweet Spot at https://bit.ly/2P2lo6X.

OTHER TITLES BY MONICA WALTERS

Love Like a Nightmare

Forbidden Fruit (An Erotic Novella)

Say He's the One

Only If You Let Me

On My Way to You (An Urban Romance)

8 Seconds to Love

Breaking Barriers to Your Heart

Any and Everything for Love

Savage Heart (A Crossover Novel with Shawty You for Me by T. Key)

I'm In Love with a Savage (A Crossover Novel with Trade It All by T. Key)

Don't Tell Me No (An Erotic Novella)

Training My Heart to Love You

To Say, I Love You: A Short Story Anthology with the Authors of BLP

Blindsided by Love

Drive Me to Ecstasy

Whatever It Takes: An Erotic Novella

Ignite My Soul

Never Enough (A Novella update of the Sweet Series Characters)

When You Touch Me

When's the Last Time?

Come and Get Me

Best You Ever Had

Deep As It Goes (A crossover novel with Perfect Timing by T. Key)

In Way Too Deep

You Belong to Me

The Shorts: A BLP Anthology with the Authors of BLP

All I Need is You (A crossover novel with Divine Love by T. Key)

Until I Met You

Marry Me Twice

Nobody Else Gon' Get My Love (A crossover novel with Better Than Before by T. Key)

Behind Closed Doors Series

Be Careful What You Wish For

You Just Might Get It

Show Me You Still Want It

Sweet Series

Bitter Sweet

Sweet and Sour

Sweeter Than Before

Sweet Revenge

Sweet Surrender

Sweet Temptation

Sweet Misery

Sweet Exhale

Motives and Betrayal Series

Ulterior Motives

Ultimate Betrayal

Ultimatum: #lovemeorleaveme, Part 1

Ultimatum: #lovemeorleaveme, Part 2

Written Between the Pages Series

The Devil Goes to Church Too

The Book of Noah (A Crossover Novel with The Flow of Jah's Heart by T. Key)

The Revelations of Ryan, Jr. (A Crossover Novel with All That Jazz by